HOKE JOHN'S LAND

HOKE JOHN'S LAND

The Bannen family embarked on a 400-mile trek to Nebraska in search of a richer and more settled life. Then when they had finally established a small homestead they were fated to feel the full force of the cattlemen's advance across the Kansas border. Hoke Bannen knew he had to make a stand and soon he was driven to shoot a few heifers in order to warn off the cattlemen. That was when his troubles really began. He fought with his fists and guns but would it be enough? Would he save his home and his family despite the odds?

HOKE JOHN'S LAND

by

Caleb Rand

Dales Large Print Books
Long Preston, North Yorkshire,
BD23 4ND, England.

British Library Cataloguing in Publication Data.

Rand, Caleb
    Hoke John's land.

    A catalogue record of this book is
    available from the British Library

    ISBN   978-1-84262-676-4 pbk

First published in Great Britain 2008 by Robert Hale Limited

Cover illustration © Gordon Crabb by arrangement with
Alison Eldred

Published in Large Print 2009 by arrangement with
Robert Hale Ltd.

Dales Large Print is an imprint of Library Magna Books Ltd.

Printed and bound in Great Britain by
T.J. (International) Ltd., Cornwall, PL28 8RW

1

Forty miles north of the Kansas border, the worn down, canvas-topped wagon lurched when one of its wheels dropped into a sandy rut.

'Look out, you goddamn buzzard baits,' Hoke Bannen shouted. The man was short-tempered at the stumbling of one of his big claybank mules.

Utensils and tools that hung from the sides of the wagon, swayed and clanked. The two short-horns that were hitched to the tailgate, bellowed fearfully and swung their heads low.

Hoke rubbed a neck cloth at the dust, smeared sweat across his face. Ahead of him, and as far as he could see, the barren land stretched to a haze of infinity. 'You got four goddamn feet each,' he yelled. 'Try stayin' on 'em.'

A few moments later he heard the voice of his wife. 'Hoke? You hearin' me, Hoke?' She was calling out from behind him.

Hoke gripped the seat iron, turned and drew the canvas flap aside. 'Can't be much longer, Coral,' he assured her. 'There's water up ahead,' he lied. 'The cows seem to know somethin'. Their eyes are just fit to pop.'

'Sam's so thirsty,' Coral said, her voice weakened with the strain of many worries.

Hoke ground his teeth, glanced at the boy sitting quietly next to her. 'You think I don't know that?' he snapped irritably. He closed the flap, cracked his whip angrily out around the head of his team. 'Give him some water, goddamnit. Give him my ration.'

The mules went into a reluctant canter, and the wagon rolled faster across the blistered soil. Hoke eyed the ground ahead of him vigilantly. If he allowed a wheel to crack, it would mean more debilitating time before they'd move again.

He jerked the reins impatiently, stared over the sweating backsides of his team. He knew there was water ahead somewhere. 'How the hell big is this place called Nebraska? Them tribes of Israel were only hexed for forty goddamn days,' he muttered, and straightaway considered telling Coral he was sorry.

They were still on a north heading, and Hoke was determined to tough it out. The steely hardness showed in his piercing blue eyes. Two years ago he'd sold everything he possessed to bring his family more than 400 miles across the State of Kansas from Oklahoma City. They sought new life with a quarter section of fertile and productive farmland. But now, after fording the Republican River, even scrub couldn't feed from the earth, and there wasn't so much as thistle weed to start a camp-fire.

Hoke shouted, and the weary mules sucked in great lungfuls of searing, arid air. Their hoofs kicked up a pall of dust that powdered

9

Hoke and masked the wagon. The short-horns heaved their ribby shoulders, extended their necks as they kept pace across the water scrape.

'If you want to drink, run for it,' Hoke yelled hoarsely. He drove on mercilessly, ripped the whip ever closer to the team's straining flanks. But, after a few minutes, he slackened the pace when he felt a hand pulling at his arm.

'Ease up, Hoke', his wife was calling. 'Ease up.' From inside the wagon, Coral was staring up at Hoke, then beyond, towards the massive sky. 'Look ahead of you,' she said, pointing. 'Look to the sky.'

Hoke was practically mesmerized as he sat watching the dirt shifting beneath the hoofs of the team. He hadn't seen that ahead, the rising heat-haze had begun to shift as grey clouds formed. There were thunderheads rolling south, straight towards them. He allowed the wagon to slow and felt the first soft swell of a preceding wind. Moments later, a silver flash sizzled along the horizon and the sky boomed.

'That'll be where the North Platte runs,' he said. 'There's a bit of a blow comin' to welcome us, Coral.'

'I'm comin' to sit out there with you,' Coral said, hearing the emotional fracture in Hoke's voice.

'Hah, you'll be in for a drenchin' inside or out,' Hoke replied excitedly. In five minutes he'd loose-hitched the mules alongside the wheels of the wagon. He hammered two stakes into the ground and stretched a canvas sheet from the tail-gate. Within seconds, the rain soaked him to the skin as he tied secure knots. The barren plain turned to muddied streams between the shallow gullies and stony ridges. He grinned, shook his fist at the sky as the rain lashed against him.

'Nebraska's baptism,' he yelled.

He cupped his hands and, as they filled, pushed them to his mouth. He pulled off his Stetson, ran his fingers across his face, through his scissor-cropped hair.

After a half-hour of the torrential down-pour, the family had enough stored water to last them another week. They travelled for another five days, until the plain gradually lost its exhausted crust, and grassy shoots and small plants began to show.

As they drew closer to the North Platte River, the ground lost its sandiness, the pasture grew green and lush. It was the middle afternoon of another three days, when Hoke turned the wagon upstream. He followed the winding course of Red Willow Creek for another five miles before he found a place shallow enough to ford. He urged the team across, the body of the wagon almost floating as the mules strained against the current.

When the nervous animals felt the shift of stones beneath their feet they faltered momentarily. 'Don't stop now, goddamnit,' Hoke shouted. 'There's a million acres o' grass an' the sweetest of all clovers waitin' on the other side.'

With their coats glistening, the team pulled up on the wide sloping bank. Hoke swung to the ground and kneeled to uproot a tuft of downy brome. 'Coral,' he shouted, squeezing a handful in his big fist. 'I think we might have got to where we're goin'.'

'Yes, Hoke, I know,' she answered quietly. Now Sam was standing on the seat alongside his mother who was looking down at Hoke. 'We're here,' she confirmed.

Hoke waved his arm, traced a line around a bend of the creek. 'There's wood for the cuttin' an' we can grow whatever we want. It's a well-protected spot. I can build us somethin' here, Coral.'

'We can plant those beans you like so much, an' taters, too. An' we'll have an apple orchard. I read somewhere it's called the Tree Planter State. What would you like, Sam?' she asked, as the boy climbed down from the wagon.

'Corn dodgers, Ma,' he shouted.

'Yeah, an' why don't that surprise me. An' where'd you think you're goin'?' Coral asked.

'He knows he don't have to eat in the wagon any more,' Hoke answered grinning.

'I never did ask what it was you got in them boxes other than seed, Coral,' he said, 'but in the trunk, among the airtights, there's some lemon sugar, an' a bottle o' ginger beer. I've been savin' 'em for such a moment.'

'Add 'em to what I squirrelled away, an' it's a banquet,' she said with a bright, happy smile.

2

The first year was long and arduous. There was much to do, and no more than two pairs of hands to do it. With a little carrying help from Sam, Hoke and Coral between them built a log cabin. They made it from green pine that Hoke felled from the surrounding timberland. They had one spacious room with a shuttered window on each side. The cracks were puddled with clay and straw. It was snug, solid with a thick-sodded roof.

Hoke fashioned a sturdy plough-staff and he cultivated and planted his crops in accord with one of his well-thumbed farming manuals. He read about the work the soil had to do, planned the furrows to hold water during the dry seasons. But it was still a struggle to survive, and the staple foodstuffs of flour, salt and molasses they'd packed into their wagon were dwindling fast.

In the second year there was a good yield of barley and corn and their food store burgeoned. Hoke had taken a hundred mile round trip to Julesburg to trade root vegetables for candy, coffee, tobacco and lamp oil. He collected a mail-order catalogue for Coral and bought a clasp-knife for himself. From the curio trader outside of town, he'd purchased a Pawnee war lance for Sam. He also returned with four hens and two roosters. Now, more than a hundred chickens scratched in their run and a dozen head of cattle grew fat off clover and sweet meadow grasses.

But Hoke never relented on his extravagant plans for the land. 'They're comin', Coral, I can almost hear 'em,' he said. 'Out o' the Dakotas, an' trainloads across from Denver, Colorado. Thick as flies on a cow's snout, they'll build new towns. But it'll be us that gets the richest an' fattest off the best an' biggest land, Coral, just you see.'

Coral listened. She was worried, didn't

want to be richest or fattest. Happiest and most contented would have suited her. She saw the craving in her husband's eyes. 'We'll be shippin' out from Ogallala to Omaha an' all points east,' Hoke went on. 'Trainloads o' quality stuff with our name on it. One day everyone'll know the name o' Bannen.'

Hoke had ambition and determination; Coral had a developing sense of misgiving. She watched Sam as he tottered about with a whittled pistol tucked into his homespun pants. 'Fightin' raiders,' he'd said, with curious portent.

Those that Hoke said would come, did. But it wasn't in the way he'd said. They weren't the farmers he'd imagined or told Coral about. They were mostly greasy sack outfits of determined, unruly men, who'd driven longhorn steers across hundreds of miles of scrub desert. They wanted grassland to swell their cattle into vast herds. Like Hoke, they were men who saw the chance of selling in the East for unimaginable wealth.

Hoke rode two miles to meet the first of them as they forded Red Willow Creek. His jaw clenched as he saw the longhorns surging across the swift running water. He reined in his mule, watched as the cattle pushed and struggled up the sloping bank.

There were three men, and they rode up to where Hoke was sitting silently on the home side of the creek.

'Nice evenin'.' It was a spare, tight-looking man riding a claybank mare, who first spoke up. Hoke looked at the man and nodded indifferently.

'I'm Tapps Morgan,' the man offered. He waved at his associates as they rode up to join him. 'This here's Jump Geigan an' Mud Foley.'

Very briefly, Hoke nodded again.

'An' you'll be Hoke Bannen,' Morgan proposed.

Hoke glared suddenly. 'Yeah,' he said, after a short delay. 'Now we've all been introduced, you can tell me what the hell them cattle are doin' here?'

'It's good cattle country,' the man responded smartly to Hoke's obvious anger.

Hoke eyed the men called Geigan and Foley. 'It's *farmin'* country, an' will be as long as I'm workin' it,' he said coldly.

Morgan looked at his men, then back at Hoke. 'I got a mixed herd o' steers. Two or three years on, there'll be near to a thousand, an' in ten years, ten thousand. They'll be larded thick as blubber. In my book, ticklin' seed stuff ain't the work o' men.'

Hoke's face darkened at the intended slight. He imagined Morgan's cattle wandering across his land, stamping down the soil, chewing up his crops. He leaned forward in his saddle. 'Listen, Morgan, I'm takin' offence to you an' your words,' he said, in grim manner. 'This is my land, so get off it. You an' your friends an' your cattle.'

The three men tensed and the thin smile slid from Morgan's face. 'You're mighty unneighhourly, Bannen,' he grated.

Hoke moved the back of his hand across his mouth, looked upstream and thought of

Coral and Sam. Then he turned back to Morgan. 'Yeah, an' you best believe it,' he said menacingly. 'Just stay away from me an' mine. That's a fair warnin'. The only one I'm givin'.'

As Hoke spoke, the man called Geigan pulled out his revolver, rested it across the top of his forearm. 'These beeves have a way of wanderin' anywhere their bellies takes 'em,' he threatened quietly.

Hoke looked at him scornfully, thought of his old guns in the trunk in the cabin. 'You threatenin' me with that piece of iron?' he challenged. 'You must've noticed I ain't rightly armed.'

'Put the gun away,' Morgan snarled at him.

With a grunt and a shrug of his shoulders, Geigan rammed his gun back into its holster. 'Don't need this to break open any tomato kisser,' he warned.

Hoke gave Geigan a hard, penetrating look. Then he dismounted slowly, let the mule stand untethered. He turned around, looked up at Geigan. 'You gettin' down, or do you want me to come up there to you?' he said quietly.

Geigan cursed as he swung down from his horse. He handed the reins to Mud Foley, unfastened his gunbelt and hung it across the horn of his saddle. He was heavy set, but it was saddle flab, not work muscle. He was making the mistake of thinking that farming really was for those who picked peaches and sucked on tomatoes.

Foley edged his horse towards the two men, but Morgan held up his hand. 'Keep out o' this, Muddy. Let's see how tough our boy really is.'

Snorting with a mix of bravado and indignation, Geigan started in at Hoke. He made a low tucked-in charge, expecting to take him hard in the belly. But Hoke dug a heel firmly into the ground and swayed to one side, swung a fist that cracked into the sharp bone of Geigan's nose.

Geigan turned into the dust, rolled over and shook his head. There was blood oozing down the front of his face, and the shame of being hit and then falling, maddened him. He sniffed, scrambled to his feet and made another run at Hoke. This time, he was caught with an arcing blow to the side of the head, and again, went reeling from the solid punch. With balled fists, he stood panting, considering his next move. He spluttered and spat, made a wary half-circle around Hoke. Then he lunged in again, the full weight of his shoulder finding Hoke's ribs. He avoided another punch and got both hands around Hoke's neck. But it was to little advantage and he took a succession of short, powerful jabs in his belly flab and his fingers loosened.

Hoke felt the pain in his ribs and he was breathing hard. But it was more from excitement than effort. Warming to his task, he raised his fists, took up the bearing of a pugilist.

A deep frown eased from Morgan's features. Now he smiled thinly at the inevitable outcome of the fight.

Foley whistled through his teeth. 'Don't look like no hay shaker to me, boss,' he muttered.

Hoke moved back as Geigan advanced. He threw two jabs at the man's flushed face and one caught him below the eye, the other square in the mouth.

'You goin' to stop this, Tapps? Jump's about to get his head pulped,' Foley yelled.

'No,' Morgan retorted with a shake of his head. 'I'm curious as to just how he's fixin' to break open this particular tomato kisser.'

Blood was roaring in Hoke's ears and he moved fast. He was reaching with his fists when he slipped. His foot twisted in a divot and he lost his balance. He staggered on the slope of the bank, then fell awkwardly, full length into the margin of the creek. He spluttered, twisted violently as the cold torrent rushed across his face.

Geigan cursed and spat from his split lip. But he saw his advantage and moved in obstinately. He jumped, forced Hoke's head back under the water with the heel of his boot. Hoke gasped and took in a great draught of water. At the same time, he grasped Geigan's leg and wrenched desperately with both hands.

Hoke stretched out an arm as Geigan crashed down beside his twisting body. He grabbed an overhanging branch of willow and lashed out a boot as he dragged himself up, gasped at the pain when his toe caught the man square on his hard jawbone.

'I can see you fought more'n hogweed in your time, feller,' Morgan decided. 'But now that's enough.'

With water dripping from his chin and fingertips, Hoke stood in the shallows, ran the flat of his hand across the top of his head. 'It'll be enough when *I* decide. That goes for *now*, or any other time,' he rasped. But he looked down at Geigan, saw the pink run of water across the man's broken face and lost interest in the fight. He put one foot up on the bank and looked Morgan straight in the eye. 'My pa told me that threatened folk should take more precautions,' he said. 'You might bear that in mind if you ever think o' visitin' me again, Morgan. Now get off my land.'

Morgan stroked his chin as Mud Foley went to have a look at Geigan. 'No doubt your pa was a prudent man,' he said. 'But I could tell Foley to shoot you right now.'

Hoke walked over to his mule. He took the reins loosely in his hand, patted its withers. He looked upstream towards his cabin, then back at Morgan. 'I don't think you'll do that,' he replied. 'Smartness or guts, you probably ain't got either.' He turned the mule around in a tight circle. 'Remember, next time you'll be up against them precautions, an' that don't mean a fist fight.'

Hoke walked off and didn't look back as the pain welled across his ribs. He wondered if Coral would have been proud of him.

3

Tapps Morgan and his men established themselves ten miles downstream. But within weeks, more small herds were fording Red Willow Creek on to new grazing land. Silent with concern, Hoke Bannen watched from a distant willow brake. He didn't make himself known, just started on the brush and wicker fencing to protect his vegetable crop. But it was a futile gesture with the extensive land holding he now had. It would have been a feasible job with posts and wire, but he couldn't afford the raw materials.

It was at the tail end of the second year that another would-be crop grower came seeking fortune. He was a good-natured immigrant named William McKluskey whom his wife fondly referred to as Irish. They possessed an all-embracing hope, but in everything else

26

were pathetically poor. When Hoke told him of the cattlemen and their increasing herds, McKluskey shook his head ruefully.

'These cattle herds sure eat up the land. Trample it good, too,' he said, from his covered brake-wagon. 'But I'm still for buildin' us our own farm. Maybe there's somethin' further along the water,' he hoped.

Hoke recognized the McKluskeys' determination, and after they'd shared supper of pumpkin pie with potatoes that the Irishman had laughed at, he wished them well as the couple set off to look upstream. 'You might still have to travel some, but I'm sure what you're lookin' for's up there,' he said hopefully.

The McKluskeys finally settled twenty miles away, close to where the Red Willow forked into the Blackwood Creek. It was little comfort for Hoke to know there was another farmer in the territory, but for Coral at least, it was another woman's company should she ever need it.

It was a couple of weeks later, and just after first light, when Hoke saw the first of the steers. It was chewing its way through a rich barley yield and it carried a Crook Water brand. The beast looked up as Hoke's lariat coiled around its heavy shoulders. Hoke dropped a hitch around his saddle horn and walked away. He rode easy, with the roped steer following on a few paces behind and, as he crossed the open rangeland he saw more loose cattle. Small bunches of short and long yearlings were close cropping the grass, steadily working their way towards his own land. He was pushing near twenty head and the sun was dipping when he came within sight of the Three Creeks camp.

It was a makeshift affair with a short bull train, had canvas stretched between the wagons. It was run by a dozen ex-army men from Fort Kearney who'd invested their meagre pensions in cattle.

Whatever it was they were doing, the men stopped, waited with open curiosity as Hoke approached. He let go of the lead steer's rope as he rode up. He dismounted slow and confident, let the mule stand its ground. 'I'll exchange what I brought in for a cup o' coffee,' he suggested calmly. 'An' which o' you fellers is the boss o' this outfit?' he added, as they stared back at him.

A swarthy, black-bearded man pushed his thumbs into his belt. 'I'm Ramsay Polman. Who are you?' he said.

'Hoke Bannen,' Hoke replied.

The man grunted. 'So. The nester from upriver who don't take to cattle. We thought you'd turn up sooner or later.'

'If that's the way you want it,' Hoke acknowledged.

Smiling sourly, the other men moved in closer and Hoke took a mug of coffee from one of them. 'Your cattle were movin' on to my land,' he said. 'Fact, one of em already started in on my barley crop. But I'll put that down to you not hearin'.'

The bearded man eyed Hoke doubtfully. 'Not hearin' what?' he asked warily.

Hoke spat the hot stewed coffee into the

ground at his feet. 'I'll fight any goddamn son-of-a-bitch who runs livestock over any part o' my land.'

'Hah, you sure got sand in your craw, feller. I'll say that for you.'

Hoke handed back the coffee. 'My purpose is just as great as yours,' he said. 'Difference is, I've got a family to support, an' I got here first.'

The man looked around him. 'I'm obliged to you, mister, for pointin' that out,' he said. 'But are you tryin' to tell us somethin'? I can't believe you're threatenin' us.'

Hoke combined a tired smile with a shake of his head. 'Public information, an' I'll stick it on a tree if you like. Next time, your cattle won't be comin' back.'

'Our poor cows don't seem to understand the grazin' rights over this land, Mr Bannen. We'd sure react badly to any harm done to any one of 'em.'

'Well they'll understand a goddamn fence,' Hoke retorted aggressively. 'Get your place wired, otherwise I'll dig 'em in as manure on mine. I ain't sufferin' for you an' your goddamn disregard.'

The man stared at the ground, thought for a moment. Then he looked up as one of the other men stepped up beside him. 'It's him who saw off Tapps Morgan,' the man said. 'I hear he made a real mess o' Jump Geigan ... seems he don't take much to sweet-talkin'.'

Hoke turned back to the man called Ramsay Polman. 'The man shouldn't've pulled a gun on me,' were his final words.

The Three Creeks men watched uneasily as Hoke climbed into his saddle. They all had time-earned money invested in their small herd and were troubled by the confrontation, at Hoke's hard-nosed warning.

'Until the next time then,' Polman muttered with conviction, but more to himself than anyone else.

The following year, the cattle multiplied as Tapps Morgan had said it would. The herds became unmanageable and Hoke found the brands and earmarks of many more outfits. It was after he'd discovered damage to his valu-able grain feed that he decided to carry out the threats he'd made to Ramsay Polman.

He selected a heifer from each of the accountable herds and drove them to where he'd had the fight with Jump Geigan. He dispatched each of the young animals with a single shot, and with their brands upper-most, laid them along the bank of the creek. On the trunk of the big, old overhanging willow, he tacked a slat with a few crudely cut words:

TRESPASSERS <u>NOT</u> FORGIVEN.
BANNEN.

It was as he'd said, but he didn't tell Coral of the sign or the sentiment. His slaughter of the cattle would have turned her against him; just as it did every cattle herder between the Republican and Platte Rivers.

Ten days later, Hoke discovered the price he'd paid. A sizeable herd was driven deliber-ately across two acres of his tenderest food crops. It wasn't a chance incident as before, it was eye-for-an-eye retribution from those whose cattle he'd put his gun to.

Hoke sat his mule until he decided his next course of action. He wouldn't single out or discriminate, he'd up the stakes. From now on, he'd shoot *every* animal that came on to his land.

4

In the weeks that followed, Hoke shot more than a dozen steers. He'd convinced himself that he killed in defence of his toil. He sought continued provision for his family, and he *had* given indisputable warning.

Then, one night in late summer, he woke to restless lowing from his pair of dairy pitchers. He moved his head on the pillow, and opened his eyes, saw the orange cast that was blooming across a side window. He rolled quickly from the mattress, was across the room in quick strides.

'Coral, get up,' he called urgently, while grabbing his boots. 'The crops are burnin'.'

Within seconds, Coral was full awake. She pulled back the canvas screen and gently shook Sam awake, got him to sit on the edge of his bed. She didn't know what was going on, and didn't want to frighten him.

'What's happenin'?' she called out. Young Sam caught the measure of distress in his mother's voice and remained silent.

Hoke turned from lighting a can lamp, and grabbed his son gently by the shoulders. 'We're goin' outside, an' I want you to run. Stay creekside ... don't go into the pasture.' he told him.

While Sam pulled on his boots, he looked at his mother then back at Hoke.

'Where to?' he asked.

'Just run, Sam,' Coral said.

Within two or three minutes Hoke had grabbed the mules. He threw Coral a coil of rope and they rode quickly. There was a night breeze that swept gently across the fields and Hoke and Coral stood the mules off a distance. Sam was swishing a heavy stick as he raced along beside the creek and Hoke yelled for him to catch up and hold the mules. He ran towards the rolling carpet of flame and the smoke swept over him, the night filling with sparks and crackling embers.

As the corn heads shattered in the heat, he backed away, tried to figure out a way of stopping the spread of fire. But knew there was nothing he could do, and he muttered a dark and fearful aftermath.

Before first light they were sitting near the creek. They were all soot-grimed, smeared with dirt and blackened ash. Her eyes red-rimmed, Coral stared out across their blackened fields. There were still traces of glowing embers close to the ground, but they were dying. She ran the palm of her hand across Sam's forehead and looked at Hoke.

'There's pages in that old manual o' yours that mentions crop burnin'. It's somethin' to do with bringin' on new growth. So it don't have to be the end,' she sniffed, smiled emotionally.

But Hoke's mind was elsewhere, because he knew that very soon, Coral would be asking what caused the fire. He closed his eyes for a moment, issued more silent and chilling retribution.

He hoisted Sam up on to one of the

nervous mules, and in silence they walked back to the cabin. Hoke lit more lamps and Coral made coffee. Sam lay on his bed, but he propped himself on his elbows, watched and waited for dawn to break.

Coral handed Hoke a large mug of strong coffee. 'Who's done this, Hoke?' she asked with quiet determination.

'Them that want the right to let their cattle graze.' With the faces of Polman, Tapps Morgan and Jump Geigan turning through his mind, Hoke told the half-truth.

'Some days you've been gone from dawn till dusk. Is that somethin' to do with *"them"*?' she asked.

'Yeah. We got the best land, an' they want their cattle on it.' Again he answered indirectly. 'An' it's only goin' to get worse.'

Coral saw that Sam had fallen asleep. She stared through the window as veins of pink, early light broke through the darkness. She was deeply troubled, disconsolate at the shift of her husband's character.

'Why do they want *our* land?' Coral wanted

to know.

'Because the pasture's rich in growth. They want it for the feed. They call us all sorts o' names,' he snapped. 'People like us an' Will McKluskey.'

Coral looked at Hoke anxiously. 'Do you think we should give all this up? We've worked for so long,' she said, stopping his outburst.

'No, Coral. I'm meanin' it won't be *us* that moves on. What happened here tonight takes care o' that. Corn ain't the only stuff that gets to grow stronger when it's burned.'

Coral placed her hand over her husband's. 'Think about Sam,' she asked of him. 'You're not tellin' me what's really been happenin', I know that much, Hoke. But I want it to stop. I want it as it *was* … as you used to be.'

Hoke walked across the cabin and pulled open the door, looked at the water as it raced along the creek. 'I never come this far to let someone break me,' he rasped. 'Hell's goin' to be froze over, before it happens again.'

There was an awkward stand-off between Hoke and Coral Bannen for many days after the fire. Hoke took to the repairing of fences and planting of the winter yield. There was no let-up in his labour. Day after day, he left the cabin at first light and didn't return until sunset. Coral didn't ask what he was expecting, but she noticed that as well as the Colt that Hoke took to carrying, the old plains rifle was now missing from the shelf above the cabin door.

The confrontation happened in the early fall when Hoke had been hoeing long rows of squashes. He got to his feet to stretch his aching muscles, saw bolts of lightning strike brilliant along the North Platte, heard the low roll of distant thunder. He looked west to where the sky was darkening, cursed loud at the broken line of cattle approaching through the clusters of low-growing peas.

It was what he'd been prepared for. He cursed confidently again and snatched up his rifle in his left hand, eased the Colt from its holster with his right. He backed off a few steps to where the soil was banked, saw the Three Creeks riders above the weaving horns of the steers.

'You ain't shootin' *these* steers, Bannen,' one of Polman's men shouted out to him. 'An' I ain't matchin' fists with you 'cause of it.'

Hoke swung up his rifle, eased back the hammer. 'Then you'll match it with whatever I've rammed down the barrel o' this ol' cannon, friend,' he returned.

The two riders exchanged a word, but one of them made the mistake of pulling his rifle. He'd meant to fire through the cattle as a warning, turn the herd around and frighten Hoke off.

But Hoke wasn't set for such gestures. He'd already fallen to his knee and fired. The man caught a heavy bullet high in the front of his chest and it blasted him from the saddle. As the cattle broke away, the second man was wheeling his horse when Hoke's second bullet ploughed across the back of his shoulders.

The cattle veered away from the gunfire and Hoke ran forward. He saw the man grimacing, his coat ripped open and already bloody.

'You ain't dead yet. Get your friend's body off my land,' he yelled. 'Rope an' dog him if you have to. He ain't goin' to suffer any shame.'

It was nearly dark when Hoke got back to the cabin. Coral and Sam were sitting on the step watching geese fly south, waiting for the rain to follow.

Hoke's weariness showed as he grabbed at the mane of his mule, swung to the ground.

'What's happened, Hoke?' she said, her voice shaking.

There was a detached gleam in Hoke's eyes, 'They came at me with a herd ... drove 'em across the goddamn pea field,' he growled. 'It was Polman's outfit. One of 'em put his gun up at me.'

A wave of fear swept through Coral as she watched Hoke playfully twist his fist against

Sam's cheek.

'Did you kill him, Hoke?' she pleaded, following him inside.

'If I hadn't've done, it would o' been *him* tellin' Polman what he did to me,' Hoke explained sharply. 'Yeah, he's dead all right.'

Coral gave Hoke coffee. 'Let's get out, Hoke. Please, before it gets any worse,' she said. 'The law's too far away, an' there's Sam to think of.'

'If we move on, they win, Coral, an' that ain't right,' Hoke said, his voice affecting and tight.

'It's nothin' to do with bein' right or wrong any more,' Coral insisted. 'It's about the worth o' things.'

'I know that. It'll be me they want now. They won't touch you or the boy.'

'Why don't you just go an' join up with 'em? You've got what it takes ... the gift to kill for what you want.' Coral slung the words out. She wasn't going to argue with her husband. She knew it was useless to try and change him once he'd decided. In that, he hadn't changed.

The first big raindrops slanted across the land as she stepped outside. 'We must have missed the geese,' she muttered, the fear and frustration gnawing inside her. Then she stood for a long time, the rain running with the tears that soiled her face.

5

A week later, and forty miles north of the Republican River, Owen Pipe reined in his horse. 'These scatterlin's want back to the home ground, Otis,' he drawled at his brother, after spitting a mouthful of tobacco juice into the dust.

Otis, a thick-set, doughy man followed the cattle with his puffy eyes. 'Yeah, don't we all. Maybe if we shocked 'em up, they'd run to the Bannen property,' he said.

Owen took a moment's thought. 'The boss said we was to ride around any trouble. Maybe we should earmark some of this stock,' he said doubtfully.

'An' Bannen?' Otis remarked.

'If he turns up, he turns up. We play that card if an' when it happens.'

Otis grunted. 'We weren't told we couldn't

defend ourselves. Bannen shouldn't've killed Lomax. An' Arkie Munce ain't ever goin' to stand up straight again.'

Owen nodded at his brother's meaning and kicked his horse towards the cattle. Together, they bunched the herd up and drove them north for about another mile. As they approached the bend in Red Willow Creek, Otis cut out a calf. The unbranded animal ploughed wildly into the Bannens' field of near-ripened wheat. It dashed and swerved, crushed out a patch that was spread wider by the yelling Pipe brothers.

Close to the centre of the pale-golden field, Otis built a loop. With a practiced throw, he hogged-down the animal and it bellowed, its eyes bulging with fear. Owen made a quick ear-crop, then they stood back and watched the young cow as it climbed shakily back to its feet.

Otis coiled his rope and walked to the creek. He looked around him, then grabbed up some dried leaves and catkins from the bank. He placed some blowdown twigs on top, then went for a handful of broken corn stalks.

Owen was curious. 'You makin' a fire, Otis?' he asked.

'Yeah, small but smoky. Maybe it'll move farmer Bannen from his pen.'

Owen shook his head. 'If there ain't any trouble, you'll make it, eh, Otis?' he said ruefully.

Otis was about to grin at his brother when the noise made him start. He was up on his feet as a horseman came beating from the high grass that verged the creek.

Both men instinctively reached for their handguns. Otis's trigger finger had taken up pressure before he realized the rider was a boy mounted on a claybank mule.

As the mule spraddled to a halt, Sam Bannen appeared to throw up an arm. There was a blur of movement and a glint, before the surprised man got hit. Owen Pipe grunted and went down on his knees. He pushed a hand out to the ground to stop himself falling further, looked down to see the shaft of a Pawnee war lance, stuck low in his belly.

'Otis, you ain't goin' to believe this,' he cried out.

Otis snatched up his rope and quickly tossed out a high loop for the boy's shoulders. He yanked hard and pulled Sam down. But they had more than a callow youngster to deal with. Sam Bannen was already hardy and resolute.

Otis looked at his brother. 'You been hurt bad, Owen?'

'Yeah, bad enough. But I'll live to kick Kid Geronimo here.' Owen winced, gasped as he pulled out the short lance.

Sam's eyes were blazing. He struggled, kicked his boots into the ground as Otis pulled up on the rope. He yelled, choking and shrill. 'Get off our land, you dirty land-grabbers.'

Owen was standing very still, his face draining of colour. He looked at the lance in his hand, his fingers sticky with blood. His features crooked up with pain and sweat beaded across his forehead. He lurched forward, pulled open the front of his pants and squinted at the bloody hole.

'We got to get you back, Owen,' Otis suggested. 'Think you're goin' to make it?'

Owen was breathing heavy. 'Yeah, long's I don't have to walk. I'm goin' to teach this...' The hurt man's threat trailed off as he glared at the boy his brother was holding down. 'You're the offspring o' that goddamn pain in the ass, sodbuster Bannen,' he snarled.

'You get out o' my pa's field,' Sam squealed with tears of shame and outrage.

'I'll give you somethin' to remember what you done to me,' Owen hissed. 'Somethin' to show the rest o' your tribe.'

'What you got in mind?' Otis asked, unsurely.

Owen's face was damp and ashen. With a low groan, he waved the point of the lance at Sam. 'I'm goin' to mark him. I'm goin' to notch the leppy calf, an' won't his pa just love it.'

Otis looked a little more uncertain. 'For

God's sake, Owen, he ain't much more'n a weaner.'

Owen's mouth twisted slow and cruel. 'He's thrown a spear into my vitals. What do you expect me to do, send him to bed without supper?' Avoiding the flailing feet, the hurt man moved closer to Sam's squirming body. With his bloodied left hand he grabbed the boy's hair, with his right, he snatched at Sam's ear, ripped out a morsel of flesh between his thumb and its pinch with the sharp tip of the lance.

There was an enraged sound from Sam as he lost part of his earlobe. Then a wretched sob, as with one punch, Owen knocked him to the ground.

'You're lucky I ain't got an iron.' Owen spat the words, and Otis backed away astonished at his brother's cruelty.

The noise from Hoke Bannen's Hawken shattered the air. The wound in Owen Pipe's belly burst open in a crimson blur as his body lifted from the ground. He was dead long before he came to earth, a mangled pile at the very edge of the wheat field.

Otis stared at the man who'd just destroyed his brother. He saw Hoke's terrible, uncontrolled anger, the certainty of his own death.

'The hurt won't last,' Hoke said, looking to his son. 'Get back to the cabin an' your ma. Leave the mule, an' don't stop till you get there.'

Hoke turned to Otis who'd made a move for his Colt. 'Oh yeah, that's the easy way out,' he said, his mouth making the shape of a thin, icy smile. He dropped the Hawken to the ground and swung down from his mule. Then he reached into his saddle trap and drew out a claw hammer.

Otis took the first driving blow to his shoulder, the next to his elbow. He howled, held out his arms in front of him. But the hammer caught him in the wrist, then the forearm. He took a step backwards, his legs buckling slowly. Hoke was relentless. He struck again, until blood started to seep through the arms

50

of Otis's heavy denim shirt, the arms and joints beneath, all pain and bruising nerves.

Otis finally went down on his knees. He futilely grabbed for the hammer as it swung towards the side of his face, used his failing muscles to drag it down. 'That's my brother you just blown apart,' he hissed. 'So just kill me, why don't you?'

'I am, mister, in case you hadn't noticed,' Hoke said, and jerked his knee up under the man's chin.

That was when Hoke heard Coral's voice, behind him.

'Stop it!' she screamed, running at him. She made a grab at Hoke, her hand striking the hammer that was wet and shiny. As he pushed her away, she saw his arm was splattered with bright blood.

As Coral fell, she clutched at Hoke's muddied boots. But her husband stepped forward, and like nailing tacks to a post, he continued to strike at Otis Pipe's body. Coral stretched out an imploring hand, and Hoke trod on her. He looked down to see her sprawled at his feet and he faltered.

'They cut him like a cow,' he stuttered breathless, shaking himself from the grip of his mind.

Coral reached up and took the bloody hammer, trembled at the warm stickiness on her fingers. She drew herself up from her knees and gently pushed him towards the creek. 'Get cooled down, then we're goin' home,' she told him.

What seemed like an age later, Coral walked slowly towards Otis Pipe. The man's clothing was soaked dark with blood from Hoke's cruel beating. The man was in shock and he looked up with fearful eyes. Coral shuddered. She felt it hard to look directly at the man, the flesh of his face and hands broken and bruised, darkly blooded.

'The man you were with deserved to die,' she said with little emotion. 'I've saved your life, an' maybe *that's* the wrong thing. So get yourself off our land an' never ever return.'

'*Someone's* comin' back, lady. Mister Polman's goin' to bring riders when he collects my brother. Dig yourselves a real deep fraidy hole.'

Coral turned away from the man, as he croaked from stinging, split lips. She fetched the two horses and handed him the reins of one of them. She watched as he pulled himself into the saddle, as he squeezed his eyes shut against the pain, then she turned away.

'We got some talkin' to do, Hoke,' she said despairingly. 'There's someone who was once a child to consider.'

Hoke was rubbing his eyes, coughing, shaking his head. He got up from his knees beside the creek, walked unsteadily away from the bank. 'It's more than the crops, Coral. I told 'em to make their choice.' Hoke's thoughts were still dark and menacing as he started off along the creek to their cabin.

'He said Polman's comin' back with more riders. What does he mean, Hoke?' Coral called out, as she followed on.

'It means that Ramsay Polman's gain' to turn a mite ungodly, Coral.' Hoke stopped and turned back to his wife. 'It ain't your way ... means you an' Sam will be movin' out.'

'I wouldn't consider that, even if there was somewhere to move to.'

Hoke was silent until they reached the cabin. 'You can take the mules an' ride north to the fork. They ain't got no quarrel with the McKluskeys. You'll be safe there.'

'No. We came this far together, Hoke, an' we're stayin'. It's where we belong.'

Sam pulled the cabin door open, and Hoke saw the dressing that Coral had tied around the side of his face. Coral knew then that her husband was right. She didn't fully understand the conflict, but she'd known of his bloody-mindedness since they'd set out from Oklahoma City, five years ago. 'So, how long before we come back?' she asked forlornly.

'A couple o' weeks. I'll come an' get you.'

It was dusk when Coral and Sam rode out in their rundown stock wagon. Coral looked up to the inky sky, saw more geese continuing their long flight south.

She turned to see Hoke watching them, stern-faced and stubborn. She waved good-bye, and didn't look at him again. Sam didn't say anything. He turned away, uncertain of why they were leaving.

6

Through a loophole in a battened shutter, Hoke Bannen watched his land. The moon would rise late, and he wanted to see its coming. He guessed that as an ex-army man, Ramsay Polman would make his move at first light.

He'd cleaned, loaded and checked his Colt and rifle. He hadn't stopped once to consider his chances of fighting off the Three Creeks men. His stance was a dilemma, though. If he moved on, they'd win, if he stayed and fought, he was a fire-brand and just as bad as they were. Hell, he concluded, as he set out the ammunition in preparation for their coming. It was his land, and quite simply, *nobody* was driving him off it.

The cabin itself was as safe and sound as it could be. Hoke reckoned that unless

Polman brought along some sort of field artillery, he could hold it forever.

There was a night chill, and Hoke lit a small fire of pine cones and twigs. But there was too much sparking and cracking and he had to damp it down. He sat and waited in the ensuing silence, checked the action of his guns again. After half an hour, he heard the cry of a whippoorwill from near the willow brakes and knew the men were coming. He moved to a side window and minutes later saw their movement above the low bank of the creek. They were in the water, and their shadows disappeared from view even as he watched. The deep, oppressive quiet of the cabin was shattered by a dull click as he drew back the hammer of his old plains rifle.

Soon, other shadows moved through the darkness. Hoke tried to make a count, thought there could be a dozen of them. From Hoke's recollection, that could be all of Polman's outfit, and he wondered if that meant there were more than just the Creeks men.

Hoke saw a lone figure appear through the darkness and make its way towards the cabin. He cursed silently, then exhaled and took aim. He squeezed the trigger, and against the reverberating crash of the Hawken, he heard a cry of distress. He thought he saw the shadow stumble, then fall to the long meadow grasses that edged the ground around the cabin.

The shot had hardly died away before the primed attackers opened up. Hoke gasped and turned away from the window as a volley of bullets struck. For nearly a minute, the cabin walls soaked up bullets, mud and straw chinking flew and the side shutters splintered apart. Then, as suddenly as it had started, the shooting stopped. In the surrounding darkness, through hanging curls of smoke, the deadly world turned quiet.

Hoke reloaded, flinched as a resinous twig spat from the not quite dead fire. He crossed to the other side window, and looked through a splintered shutter. He levelled the sights of his rifle, wondered if he'd see a flash from one of his attackers' carbines. But there was no more firing for the remainder of the long, bleak hours of the night. They'd got him bottled-up, and Hoke knew that who-ever was out there could bide their time.

When dawn eventually broke, Hoke was weary and gritty-eyed as he peered out again. There was a wedge of land between his pole corral and the creek, but alongside the willows, he could see the outline of a Three Creeks cooster. Huh, so it was Pol-man and his men, and they were moving in on him, using the small wagon as a rolling shield.

Hoke gently pushed against the shutter, but immediately realized his mistake. When a shattered board dropped away from its hinge, half-a-dozen carbines blasted their rounds into the cabin. Hoke hunkered down, cursed loudly as a bullet smashed one of Coral's hanging pictures.

Throughout the remainder of the day, there was sporadic pot-shotting from Polman's men. Some were covered by the cooster, others had taken vantage points around the cabin. Occasionally, one of them got careless, and Hoke loosed off a round from the Hawken. Towards first dark, he was hit. The bullet ripped through the breached shutter and raked his neck. It wasn't a wound that crippled him, but it was difficult to staunch the flow of blood and the shock drained his ebbing strength.

During the second night, Hoke considered his predicament again and again. He was thinking about what would happen to Coral and Sam if he got killed, or, as looked more likely, *when* he got killed. He knew there was no chance of him defeating Polman and his men – there never really had been. In the early, daunsy hours, when Polman's relentless strategy started to bite and Hoke was drifting into an exhausted sleep, a voice broke up the flat, pre-dawn stillness. Hoke shuddered, shook himself vigilant.

'Hey, Bannen. Can you hear me?' Ramsay Polman was calling out.

Hoke sat with his back up against the

cabin wall, winced at the pain in his neck. 'Yeah, I can hear you, Polman,' he answered hoarsely and pushed himself to his feet. 'I'm waitin' for one o' your gutless wonders to face me head on.'

'Won't happen. Forget it, Bannen. You ain't killin' any more o' my men.'

Hoke muttered a threat, eased back the hammer of the Hawken.

'If I've a mind to, Bannen, my boys'll burn you out o' there,' Polman went on. 'But I'll be losin' me a decent line shack, so don't be a dog in a manger. Get out now.'

'This place'll be yours only when I'm plum full o' bullets, Polman. I ain't movin'.'

'Listen to me, Bannen. The law in Julesburg's goin' to hang you for what you did to Owen Pipe. You can take your chance with his brother, but this way, you get your life for your land.'

'I told you, I'm stayin',' Hoke repeated.

There was silence for a while, as though a hurried whispered conference was taking place. 'You've got until sundown, Bannen.

Then I *will* burn you out,' Polman shouted finally.

'Then tell the man you send to do it, you'll be forwardin' his pay,' was Hoke's response to the man's ultimatum.

After that, as the hours of the day passed, Hoke's spirit withered. He noticed every poignant keepsake and chattel they'd accumulated since arriving from Oklahoma City. And his torment turned to anger, as he thought of Polman burning down his home. But he wouldn't quit. Everyone knew it, and that included Coral and Sam. He'd die on the front step, after killing the man who lit the first match.

Heavy clouds had formed in the east and the sun had fallen below the distant horizon, when Polman issued his farewell. 'Time to make your peace, Bannen.'

'I'll see you in Hell,' Hoke muttered defiantly. With the heel of his hand he smashed out the remains of the window shutter, then emptied his Colt at Polman's wagon.

As he reloaded, he heard a scuffle. It was

outside and somewhere near the window on the opposite side of the cabin. He cursed and banged the Colt against his leg. He'd made the mistake Polman thought he would. In his angry retaliation, he'd now been positioned. They'd drawn his fire while one of them fired the cabin on his blind side.

He swore, foul and terrible. 'Sorry, Coral. As the armed defender of our stronghold, I'm makin' one hell of a good turnip farmer,' he rasped.

7

Within ten minutes Hoke could hear the flames crackling, licking at the walls. He could see the glow from the chink above the side window.

When the heat increased, he dipped his neck-cloth in a water jug. Then he soaked his old range hat, replaced it and pulled the brim low. For a moment he considered Polman's offer, recalled how it was you lived to fight another day. But running away wasn't in Hoke Bannen's character. He wouldn't die without a fight, and he wasn't getting burned alive. So more than one Three Creeks cowman would be paying an ugly price for it.

He looked up and saw flames encircling the chimney hole. He wondered if the parched sod roof would burn as the smoke started to reach down. It curled thick on the inside of the cabin and his eyes were prickly with sweat, and he coughed.

He unlatched the door and breathing deeply he stood there. Holding the Hawken in his left hand and the Colt in his right, he thought for a second then let the Hawken drop. He wondered how far he'd get, if he'd get a chance to take Polman.

The cattlemen were waiting. When flames from the roof and walls of the cabin leaped into the night sky, they knew it wouldn't be long before Hoke Bannen broke out.

From behind the wagon, Polman kept watchful. 'Won't be long,' he said. 'Must be hotter'n a dutch oven, in there.'

As well as most of the Three Creeks men, Tapps Morgan and Mud Foley were gathered on Bannen land. They had accepted Polman's offensive, mainly because of the man's ex-army authority. There would be others who would probably understand Hoke Bannen's right to defend his family home, certainly wouldn't hold with the wanton mutilation of a child. Whereas Jump Geigan, Arkie Munce and the stove-up Pipe brother had personal grievances to settle,

'If he comes out unarmed, let him be. If not, shoot him,' Polman instructed his men.

The men trained their guns on the cabin. They pondered on the engagement, the problem of Hoke Bannen and the ferocious beatings he'd meted out. But they'd heard Polman offer him a way out, and if the man wanted to go the same way as his crops, he could.

From beneath the flames, the searing heat was now splitting the logs of the cabin. The men were so engrossed in waiting for Hoke Bannen to appear before them, that they didn't notice William McKluskey's mare and its rider.

Tapps Morgan did though. He turned, and keeping low, ran to grab the reins as the horse galloped up to the cooster wagon. He pushed his Colt back into his holster, used both hands to pull the mare's head down.

Ramsay Polman was torn between watching the cabin and Morgan. Then, in the radiance of the flames he saw who the rider was. 'Sweet Lord, it's his wife,' he faltered, recognizing Coral Bannen.

Coral flung herself from the horse and gripped the tailgate of the wagon. 'Where's my husband? Where's Hoke?' she rasped, staring at the blazing inferno.

'We're tryin' to burn him out,' Polman said as he approached.

'He's in the cabin?' Coral cried, lashing out at Polman. 'Who are you, what the hell are you doin' here? What have you done?' She was screaming uncontrollably and ran for the front of the cabin. 'Hoke, it's me, come out o' there. I've come back, Hoke,' she yelled, the words rattling from her throat.

One of the men made a move to go after her, but Polman held him back. 'Leave her,' he said. 'If he's still able, he'll come out.'

The men watched as Coral ran desperately. They sucked in hot, sooted air, gripped their guns as an explosion of sparks and flying embers, crashed around the cabin door. Coral was outlined by the billowing flame, faltered from the heat as Hoke stumbled on to the step. His eyes were blinded by smoke and fumes, and he fired blindly ahead of him into the night.

'No, don't shoot,' Polman yelled over the gunfire.

But he was too late. Before Hoke touched ground, his men delivered a single, tight volley. They saw the farmer throw up his arms when he saw his wife, as their bullets struck, and Coral stretched out to her husband. Coral staggered, and Hoke threw his Colt to the ground as he rushed to meet her. He was pulling her to him before Morgan and Polman got halfway to them.

More men came forward, but stood off uneasy as Hoke lifted Coral from the hard-packed dirt. They waited speechless as he carried her to where the reflections of the flames danced across the creek.

Polman was taking in the tragedy, waited a

moment before speaking. 'It was *you* we came for, Bannen,' he said. 'None of us ever wanted this to happen.'

Hoke knelt in the sanctuary of the cool grasses. He held Coral in his arms, looked out across the silvery, fast-running water. 'But it did,' he murmured oddly.

One of the Three Creeks' riders picked up Hoke's Colt. He glanced blankly at the blazing cabin, then at Polman. He wondered if he was the only one who'd not fired when Hoke came through the door.

Polman looked uncomfortably at Hoke. 'You'll do whatever you have to, Bannen, I know that,' he said. 'If you need any help, my men...'

Tapps Morgan touched him on the arm. It stopped him, suggested he'd said enough.

But Hoke hadn't heard what Polman had said. He was staring hard into Coral's face. Deep inside him, something was breaking up.

Polman realized it and turned to Morgan. 'This is real bad,' he said thoughtfully. 'The boys had best ride out after they've bunched up Bannen's livestock. We'll stay till daybreak.'

Throughout the long night, Hoke and Coral Bannen's cabin had burned to the ground. As darkness lifted, Polman and Morgan watched clouds of pale ash drift across Red Willow Creek. They sat with their backs against a cooster wheel, talked quietly, and passed a whiskey bottle between them.

Shortly after first light, Hoke started to dig a grave. It took two hours of heart-rending work before he finally laid down flat stones from the creek bed. He had one look towards the two cattlemen, then he walked slowly to the smoking ruins of the cabin. For a while he poked around in the embers, then he returned to the grave. He placed a small, sooted wrist bangle on top of the stones, stared down with numbed emotion.

To Polman, Hoke Bannen's grief was palpable. Standing beside Morgan, he felt surprising shame as he watched Hoke walk to the stock wagon that Coral had driven back.

'I can't take much more o' this,' Polman said, and walked forward slowly. He started to shiver as sweat ran icily between his shoulder blades.

From the seat of the wagon, Hoke turned to face him. 'If you don't put a bullet in me now, you'll *never* have a moment's peace. Not until I kill you,' he said, his voice bleak and pitiless.

But Polman felt no imminent danger. To him, Bannen looked and sounded like he was already a dead man. He glanced at Morgan, nodded for him to retrieve Hoke's Colt from the back of their cooster. 'Where's that kid o' yours?' he asked. 'We'd all feel a lot safer knowin'.'

Hoke didn't answer right away, just watched Morgan as he approached with the Colt. Polman nodded and Morgan handed up the big, old .44. Hoke eased back the hammer and turned the cylinder. He glanced at Polman and let the hammer down slowly.

'He's with the McKluskeys. An' in two or three years, you're goin' to know a lot o' fear, Polman.' Hoke's eyes were bloodshot, his face was raw, blackened with smoke and his clothes were bloodstained. He reached for the reins, held them loosely in his big, dirty hands. 'His name's Sam. Pay him for the animals and what's left o' the crop,' he said firmly. 'Tell him somethin' of his ma. You owe him that,' he added with biting contempt.

'I'll tell him, Bannen. I can see you ain't got anythin' left.'

'If I had, you'd be dead already.' With that, Hoke flicked the reins and turned the wagon. He forded the creek, then faced the mules south, towards Kansas and the Smoky Hills.

Morgan stood sideways on to the rising sun, gave a loud sigh and spat at his feet. 'One goddamn homesucker who won't be givin' us any more trouble,' he suggested.

Polman cracked a thin smile. 'Oh no, Tapps,' he returned with a slow shake of his head. 'Bannen knows as well as I do that I should've put a bullet in him ten minutes ago.'

8

'Shady Lady Springs. The funniest name in the whole o' Kansas,' the driver of the freight wagon, yelled. 'Outside o' the Bearberry Saloon, there ain't no shade for ten miles, there's never been a lady within fifty, an' you got to ride for another five if you're wantin' fresh water.'

Hoke Bannen pushed the palms of his hands against the hard-sprung seat, eased the judder from the rutted dirt and eyed the town. 'Huh. You been waitin' to get that off your chest, ever since we left Tribune,' Hoke pitched back.

'Yep, it's been a pleasure chewin' the dog with you, mister,' the driver growled. Then he grunted, and spat a gob of juice over his side of the wagon. 'I just ain't used to company,' he cackled. 'Rode with a trapper once, never

74

said a word for three days. Found out later he'd been dead for two of 'em.'

Hoke turned back to the town. Most buildings were of Kansas brick, others were lumber framed with false-fronts. For those who had them, the windows were coated with sallow dust that had blown straight off the Smoky Hills. Up on the bleached board-walk, a patch-eyed dog slung its tail between its legs, skulked low as the freighter pulled up outside the saloon. An aged miner eyed Hoke, but he wasn't partial to what he saw and dropped his eyes; like the dog, looked elsewhere.

Hoke slung his blanket-roll and slicker over one shoulder and swung to the ground. He watched the freighter as it moved off along the street, then he stepped up to the boardwalk. He was wearing hickory pants, a faded blue shirt and a skin jacket. His old range hat was sweat-stained, his face was unshaven and dirt crusted.

He fingered a silver dollar deep in his pocket, then he pushed open the doors of the saloon. It was sweltering inside and the warm moist air closed around him. It smelled of sour beer and stale tobacco, but the freighter driver was right about the shade it offered.

At one table, three men sat with a whiskey bottle, and behind the long bar that ran the length of the room, a bartender was drying glasses. 'You look like a beer an' whiskey feller,' he suggested with a slick grin.

'Don't let the look fool you,' Hoke said off-handedly, as another man caught his eye.

Against a side wall, a gambler with a bent back was perched on a bar stool. He was at a green baize-topped table, idly flipping a pack of cards.

Hoke rubbed at the tight skin on the side of his neck; for a moment watched the casual movements of the man's fingers. He crossed to the table, laid his dollar on the green cloth. 'I'll cut you for the high card,' he proposed.

The gambler's eyes flicked to Hoke's face,

made a quick study of the hard, tough features. 'Have we met before ... some other place?' he queried.

'It's possible, if you've been where I've been,' Hoke answered dismissively.

The gambler shrugged uneasily, and set out the deck.

Hoke dropped his traps to the floor, put out a big hand and fingered the deck. He shuffled awkwardly, set the cards down and waited. The gambler sniffed and cut the eight of diamonds. Without hesitating, Hoke flipped over the king.

The gambler laid a silver dollar beside the first one. 'You win,' he said with a flat voice.

'Cut again,' Hoke suggested, and smiled thinly.

The gambler riffled the cards, watched closely as this time Hoke turned a black king. He hesitated, tapped his fingers restlessly on the top card, then cut the ten of diamonds. 'Gettin' closer,' he said, and laid two more silver dollars beside the two in front of Hoke. His eyes moved restlessly. 'If you're wantin' to go on, we'll get a clean deck,' he said. 'I been shufflin' these for an hour.'

'Leave 'em,' Hoke's voice was quick and hard, stopped the movement. 'They're a tad grubby, but a little dirt never hurt anyone. Unless they're the hands of a farmer, o' course.'

The gambler's eyes moved involuntary to Hoke's own hands. 'There's somethin' about you, mister,' he said. 'You certain we ain't met somewhere?' There was a faltering edge to the man's voice and he looked over to the bar.

Hoke caught the movement. 'Right now, I ain't certain of anythin' except raisin' a stake,' he said. 'If you're a house player, losin' more'n three times is mighty careless.'

After the fourth cut, the crook-backed gambler wiped the back of his hand across his forehead. He took another penetrating look at Hoke, self-consciously moved off his stool. Then, the men who'd been drinking whiskey got to their feet, moved aside when a tall, lean man stepped forward.

'I ain't in business to bankroll you, mister. You've had your bit o' fun, but now the table's closin',' he said.

Hoke looked at the table, scooped up the two piles of silver dollars that were laid on the baize. 'I guess you got your reasons,' he said and shrugged stoically.

The man nodded. 'Join me for a drink?' he asked with an open smile.

Hoke glanced sideways at him. 'No, thanks,' he said, and glanced at the bartender. 'One slug o' your varnish, an' I probably won't live to spend my sixteen dollars,' he said, and returned the smile as best he could.

'Hmm, I was wonderin' why you stayed dry,' the man said. 'I'm Milroy Peggler, an' this is my saloon.'

The bartender pulled a wry face and reached under the bar. Hoke watched his malt whiskey being poured.

'I help myself to two weeks' pay, an' you're invitin' me to bend an elbow. Why's that?' he asked.

Peggler poured his own drink. 'I like the way you handle yourself ... quittin' before your luck runs out.'

'Hah, if only you knew, Mr Peggler.' In one long slow draught, Hoke drank the good whiskey and Peggler immediately topped it up. Hoke shook his head, and picked up his blanket-roll. 'Your card player, you called him Arkie?'

'Yeah, Arkie Munce. I don't think he makes a secret of it.'

'Hmm. Maybe he should. Ask him if he remembers Hoke Bannen. Had a wife an' kid ... worked a piece o' farmin' land up in Nebraska.'

Peggler suddenly eyed Hoke with more interest. 'Stay, an' you can ask him yourself.'

'You got somethin' on your mind?' Hoke responded to what sounded more like a proposition than an idle suggestion.

'Oh, I've always got that,' Peggler agreed and tried the open smile again. 'It's known' how to make it work for you that matters.'

Hoke looked down at his cracked, dusty boots. Out of the corner of his eye, he saw the dog lying with its nose under the batwing doors. He knew its dark-brown eyes had followed him from the moment he'd walked through the doors of the saloon.

Hoke walked slowly back to the card table. He turned his back on the small number of other customers and sat down. 'If I take another whiskey, perhaps you'll tell me what it is that's on your mind,' he said to Peggler.

Peggler collected the bottle of whiskey from the bartender and followed Hoke to the table. 'Well, there is a job that someone like you might be interested in. Especially someone who knows of Nebraska an' its land.'

'What makes you think I know anythin' o' Nebraska?'

'Because you're the feller you just been talkin' about ... Hoke Bannen.'

'What job?' Hoke asked without rising to Peggler's conjecture.

'Takin' a party north, out o' state, up to the Platte rivers.'

Hoke looked surprised. 'An' what's *your* interest?'

'Provisions ... material supplies,' Peggler said with a short laugh.

'You own a chandlers?'

'Just about. It really ain't that profitable. You are Hoke Bannen?' Peggler asked.

Hoke took an appreciative sip at his drink. 'The name's John ... Hoke John,' he said, after a moment's hesitation, but didn't offer anything more.

'Well, I guess a lot o' things have changed ... like civic improvements. Shady Lady Springs ain't changed much in the thirty years since they pulled it out from under a stone, *but it will.*'

Hoke nodded. 'Yeah. You'll plant a spreadin' chestnut tree, ask for a license on Lily Langtree's name, an' drill for water.'

'I heard it's now an offence to carry a

firearm in Dodge City.'

'It's been a while since I was there,' Hoke said.

Peggler eyed him with interest. 'Good to see there's some wit to your language, Mr John.' The saloon owner topped up Hoke's glass, then continued, 'These pilgrims ain't quite so. But they're mule-headed, an' if they stick together, they'll get through. That's their credo.'

Hoke nodded a comprehending smirk. 'An' their want is your gain?'

'It ain't just them an' theirs. The railroad's promised to run a spur, for *anyone* who guarantees a big enough turnover in supplies. Think about it, Mr John ... movin' to a land where everythin' ain't wind-worn or dust-coated. A garden of Eden, that's new an' green an' fertile.'

Hoke was thinking about it. It was near to his thinking of fifteen years ago, when he'd set out from Oklahoma City, with Coral and Sam. He sat impassively, listened to the keenness of Milroy Peggler. 'I ain't interested. I woke up from that dream,' he said. 'Anyways, most o' the country in between's been charted. You don't need my help to reach that particular happy valley.'

Peggler suddenly took a closer, more perceptive look at Hoke. 'I suspect that Arkie Munce has got somethin' to do with that decision,' he said. 'But I ain't pushin'.'

Hoke felt his heart beating faster at Peggler's picture of what was waiting in Nebraska. There were still words that echoed in his head, words that rekindled the anger and loathing he still held for the Nebraska cattlemen.

Peggler took a diversion from the personal track he'd been going down. 'There's law west o' the Missouri, an' telegraph an' press offices,' he explained. 'I'm hopin' we won't need the big ol' Colt you're parkin' under your skin coat. It's more my instinct about *you*, Mr John.'

Hoke enjoyed Peggler's awareness, considered his reasoning. 'On the far side o' the Smokies, instincts ain't much good up against dust storms an' mosquitoes. When you have to pick berries an' dig for roots after the breed stock's been eaten.' He drained his whiskey, placed the glass carefully on the table. 'But bearin' all that in mind, what sort o' pay you offerin'?'

'This is important. It means a lot to me, Mr John, so I'll pay you top dollar. But if your mind's made up already, tell me an' be done with it. You can take the next freighter out o' town.'

'Right now, top dollar means a lot to *me*,' Hoke responded. 'I can get 'em to the Republican ... even across it, but I won't be obliged after that.'

'You won't be.'

'An' if we don't leave within the week, you'll have to forget goin' anywhere 'til next spring.'

'We'll be ready. There's a few folk I'd like you to meet before we leave.'

'Who?'

'One or two who've got some idea o' what they're after. A meetin'll get 'em involved, an' you'll want to be introduced to each other.'

Hoke nodded in dubious agreement. 'Do you carry a gun, Mr Peggler?' he asked.

Peggler laughed. 'I will be, if that's your meanin',' he replied enigmatically and rose from the table. 'There's a boardin'-house down the street. Take a room after you get yourself cleaned up. Go an' see Max Plums at the stable. He'll pick you out a good horse, an' give you a Winchester. Buy any-thin' else you need, an' charge it to me.'

Hoke looked around for his bedroll and slicker, saw the dog still watching him. 'I haven't actually said I'm goin' anywhere yet, Mr Peggler.'

'You probably ain't a man to shake on a deal, Mr John, but I think you have,' Peggler said. 'How about we meet here, same time tomorrow. There's a room behind.'

As Hoke left the saloon, the clock on the back bar started its noon chime, and, guf-fawing thirstily the first of the day's drinkers pushed past him. 'Ever thought there must

86

be somethin' else out there?' he muttered at the patch-eyed dog. Then he stepped from the boardwalk and made his way to a beanery at the end of town.

9

At noon the following day, Hoke was standing under a big tent roof, out back of the saloon. There were five other men there beside Milroy Peggler, who started off the talk.

'There's twenty-five trail-worthy wagons, an' they're ready to leave within a week. Countin' these fellers, there's thirty able men, fifteen women an' six youngsters.'

Hoke looked at the men around him who were nodding agreeably at the estimation.

'Every wagon's goin' to be drawn by two mules,' Peggler continued. 'We're takin' thirty horses, an' two hundred head o' cattle. There'll be some hogs an' chickens, to.'

Peggler made his way through a wide-ranging schedule. When he was done, he told the men he intended to employ Hoke as wagon-master. 'Perhaps you'd like to say somethin' appropriate,' he said as he introduced Hoke.

'Well, I ain't ever been called "wagon-master" before,' Hoke started off, 'an' I ain't *too* sure it says a heap about this journey. We ain't headed for a clambake. Most o' you's goin' to get ill, an' some o' you'll want to turn back. At worst, some of you won't make it ... you'll die. You'll spend a lot o' your time fightin' for survival an' a lot of it recoverin'.' Hoke gave each man a steady, holding look. 'Remember, gettin' you there's *my* problem, an' I will. Stayin' there's *yours*. Get *that* schedule into your heads, an' tell your women an' children.'

The men exchanged glances, and Hoke allowed them a few, guarded words before he continued. 'We'll make up the rules as we go along, an' most of 'em will be mine. You probably won't like 'em, but they'll hurt a lot less than some o' the other stuff you'll come by.' Hoke shot a moot glance at Peggler. 'I've told Mr Peggler that my employ gets you across the Republican, but you'll do it my way.'

Another man spoke up this time. 'Are you meanin' rule of the gun, Mr John?'

Hoke nodded briefly. 'Yeah, occasionally. Try a journey without, an' see what happens. But let's not get too down about all this law-enforcement stuff. Mr Peggler assures me you'll build a fine, new town an' make a fortune ... so it's all goin' to be worth it.'

The long forgotten irony of those words made Hoke's heart thump, but he carried on. 'At least you've got some idea of how the train's got to run. If you don't like it, find someone else,' was his proposal.

Milroy Peggler got to his feet and nodded enthusiastically. 'Mr John has told you how it's goin' to be, an' I'm sure there's none of us would want it any other way. We just hadn't been prepared for – how should I say – such resolute style?'

The men looked uneasy, and Peggler turned to Hoke. 'If you could give us a minute or two, Mr John. We want the wagon-train to run on a self-governin' basis. So I just need to confirm with them that they *won't* be findin' someone else.'

Hoke accepted Peggler's roguish smile. 'I'll be in the bar finishin' your whiskey,' he said.

The patch-eyed dog was still lying with its nose under the saloon door. When Hoke walked up to the bar it looked up, flicked the last few white inches of its black tail. Hoke gave it the nearest thing he could to a conspiratorial smile, and took the tendered glass of whiskey from the barman. As was his custom, he stood watching for the unexpected, and after five minutes, Peggler appeared and indicated that Hoke rejoin him.

The five wagon men looked warily at Hoke, but Peggler looked more confident. 'There was a hitch over your idea o' discipline,' he said, 'but now we more fully understand the nature o' the task ahead, there *ain't*.'

'Oh, there will be,' Hoke muttered to himself.

Peggler moved closer to Hoke. 'Incidentally, bein' your paymaster means I no longer call you mister,' he said, as the others made straight for the street. 'An' get us a table.'

'It's a long while since I had me a first name,' Hoke said, when Peggler returned with another bottle of labelled whiskey.

'That's one way to keep it off a bullet,' Peggler said, and a moment later, Hoke smiled.

'Have you thought about what's needed in the way of extras?' Peggler asked.

'Yeah. A canvas-topped stock wagon with two cases o' bang juice, fifty rounds of ammunition for everyone that's got a firearm, an' a driver.'

'I'll see to it.' Peggler raised an eyebrow at the demand, but Hoke reckoned it was probably more to do with another bite into profit. 'Bearin' in mind what you were sayin' about gettin' ill, do you reckon we ought to be takin' a doctor with us?'

Hoke thought, then shook his head. 'There ain't too much a pill roller can do for you if the pox strikes. Sepsis an' belly bugs can be taken care of with a bone saw or scour pills. If anythin' else lays you low, you probably ain't goin' to make it in any case.'

'Somethin' for us all to look forward to, eh, Hoke?'

'Yeah, somethin' for everybody,' Hoke said. 'If you've got two men who are reliable, ask 'em to meet me here tonight. It's to talk routes an' means, so they don't have to be that smart. An' if you've got maps o' the territory, bring them too.'

'You already got a trail in mind?' Peggler asked eagerly.

'Only one to avoid,' Hoke responded sharply. 'I'm goin' to get me some sleep, then I'm takin' the patch dog for a bowl o' frontier supper.'

'What's frontier supper?' Peggler asked, looking confused.

'Somethin' I had yesterday. I thought he might appreciate it more than I did.'

Peggler laughed, and, for maybe the second time in ten years, a smile appeared on Hoke's face.

10

The wagons gathered on the outskirts of Shady Lady Springs. It was an hour after sun up, and the train wound itself in a slack line through the corrals and freighter pens. Most of the canvas-topped schooners carried a family of three or four, some of them six or seven. There were a few smaller wagon carts that were less well appointed and driven by younger, single men.

Hoke nudged his horse slowly around the column. He was looking for problems, his eyes missing very little that was outside of the wagons. As he rode, he found it difficult to stop his mind straying back to Oklahoma City all those years ago.

After a few minutes, he stopped by one wagon. He leaned from the saddle, looked closely at a mule with a streaming nose. He looked across at the driver. 'Your mule ain't well,' he told the man. 'Unhitch it an' get it away from the other animals. Buy yourself another, an' check that it's sound.'

'Bit of a summer sniffle, that's all, Mr John. It'll get us to where we're goin'.'

Hoke shook his head. 'Destroy it,' he ordered.

The driver started to protest, but he recalled a recent warning about the style of Hoke John. 'I'm goin' back into town,' he called out, as he climbed down from his wagon seat. 'Kibbs, take that goddamn mule out aways an' shoot it.'

Hoke nodded his approval and moved on. Further down the line, he stopped again. He looked down at the feet of another mule. 'There's a hoof needs repairin',' he pointed out to the driver.

'We know,' said the man's wife who was sitting next to him. 'We can't afford any more expense.'

'Take it in to the blacksmith, ma'am. Ask him to put in a staple, an' get it charged to

Milroy Peggler. Be back here in an hour.'

Hoke looked at the driver. 'You travellin' with anythin' else that's broke?' he asked.

'Nothin' I'm prepared to tell a wagon master about,' the man replied with a straight face.

'Just remember we ain't got a field hospital,' Hoke said drily, touched his hat and moved along.

There were a few more delays, mostly involving livestock or foodstuff for the animals. It was close to eight o'clock before the wagons were ready to roll.

Dixie Tennon and Jack Lambeth were the two reliable men that Hoke had spoken to earlier about routes, and he'd already sent them ahead as path-finders. Their main task was to look for trouble, possible difficulties, and report back. Hoke had also agreed to talk with the train's five representatives each evening before supper to consider their progress.

Milroy Peggler walked his sorrel mare up close to Hoke. At the head of the train, they looked back at the canvas-topped wagons. With a sudden thought, Hoke looked about him for the patch-eyed dog, 'Well, if you want to go to Nebraska...' he said, suggesting that Peggler move out.

Excited drivers flicked their whips and jiggled the reins. They called encouragement to their mule teams, as wheels creaked with their first rolling movement. Within fifteen minutes, the wagon-train was at the outskirts of town, beginning to snake its way north. Two flank riders whooped, and the small herd of cattle stirred into a steady, brawny walk.

A youngster galloped his horse to the head of the train. He pulled in and slowed to a walk alongside Peggler. 'Everythin's goin' to be new, Mr Peggler,' he said excitedly.

But it was Hoke who called across to him. 'What's your name, boy?' he wanted to know.

'Arno Rice, sir.'

'How old are you?'

'I'll be fourteen, next birthday, sir.'

'Well there ain't much that's new, Arno. Most of it's just been forgotten.' With that, Hoke suddenly kick-heeled his horse. He rode to point, a few hundred yards ahead of the train.

Arno was looking uncertainly at Peggler. 'What did he mean, Mr Peggler?' he asked.

Peggler shrugged. 'Somethin' he's dragged up from deep. But don't go askin' him, kid. Don't ever do that.' Peggler turned his horse and, as he rode back along the line of wagons, he wondered if he would ever find out what it was that Hoke John held deep inside him.

With sound wagons and fresh, healthy animals the train made good passage, nearly a hundred miles in the first few days. As they moved north, the land slowly changed, the plains becoming more undulating. As they skirted west of the Smoky Hills, the grass became more abundant. It grew richer and the cattle took up a nooning graze.

At night camp, the mules and horses were

hobbled and blankets spread. The dried contents of a chip sack were emptied on to brushwood stacks and fires were lit. Folk sat around eating biscuits and roasted meats. Some of the migrants sang songs or played musical instruments; most of them talked excitedly of the future.

But Hoke took no part. Friends and family feeling wasn't his way. After his nightly meetings with Pennon and Lambeth and the travellers' spokesmen, he sat alone, held his own council. It was only when they broke camp in the early mornings, that he moved among them to check for any potential trouble.

They'd been a week on the trail when Dixie Tennon reported a broken wheel back down the line. The wagon was almost pitched on its side. One of the large rear wheels was shattered and half its spokes were broken. The wheel hub had ploughed into the ground, and the strain had wrenched the braces and rear axle.

Hoke had a quick look. 'What the hell've

you got in that wagon?' he growled at the driver.

'Nothin' we didn't travel across half o' Kansas with,' the man said. 'Trouble is, we ain't carryin' a spare wheel.'

Hoke turned to Dixie Tennon. 'Get some help. Take the good wheels an' get 'em slung under some o' the other wagons. Put the mules behind the stock wagon.' Hoke then looked back to the driver. 'If you can find anyone who's got the space, divide up the things you want to keep. You'll have to leave the rest.'

'No need, Mr John. I can get the wheel repaired in a few hours.'

Hoke cursed under his breath. 'It's the price you're goin' to pay for a crook wagon. So, unless you reckon on puttin' up a stake notice, you an' your family can travel in some o' the other wagons.'

The driver was irked at Hoke's ultimatum. 'Apart from the wheel, this is a fine, solid wagon, an' I ain't havin' you bust it apart,' he said.

Hoke was considering how to play the man, when Milroy Peggler rode up. He was with Tennon who had three other men with him.

'Take the good wheels,' Hoke said.

Peggler contemplated the situation, eyed Hoke thoughtfully, then rode off.

From beside the broken-down wagon, the driver looked up at Hoke. 'I could catch you up sometime tomorrow,' the man said, standing his ground, stubbornly. When the men started to unload the family's chattels, his hand edged towards a small Colt he carried high and tight around his waist.

Hoke saw the threat. 'It's already goin' to be difficult for your family, mister. Don't go makin' it any worse for 'em,' he said flatly.

Dressed in plain homespuns, the man's wife stood back. She was quiet and miserable as she clasped their little girl's shoulders. For fifteen minutes they watched as some of the best of their belongings were shared around the few wagons that passed by.

'That wagon cost me an' mine just about every-thin',' the man said.

Hoke knew all too well about what things cost, something near to what the man was feeling, but he sat his horse in silence. When the wagon was nothing more than a wasted marker along the trail, Hoke told the man to take one of the rear wagons.

'I'll take care o' the niceties,' he said, understanding the anger that showed in the tightness of the man's features.

Ten minutes later, the stock wagon drew near and Hoke nodded at the driver.

'We're bein' followed. Been with us since we left Shady Lady,' the man said, indicated that Hoke look back along the trail.

About a half-mile distant, the patch-eyed dog was taking a zig-zag course. At a steady, easy lope it was obviously pursuing the train.

'Never had me a dog before,' Hoke muttered, and an hour later, he was back at the head of the train.

'A couple o' capable men *could've* repaired

that wagon,' Peggler said as he rode up. 'It wouldn't have taken more'n three or four hours.'

'Yeah, I know it,' Hoke replied. 'But we got two dozen wagons in this train. Sooner or later there's goin' to be more breakdowns, an' we ain't even made it to rough ground,' he said. 'We can't hold up, every time a wagon cracks. This way, we get some replacement wheels an' an axle.'

Peggler listened and thought over Hoke's reasoning. 'Is it that important for us to save a few hours, a few days, even? An' at the risk of soundin' tiresome, why are we savin' stuff if we ain't stoppin'?'

'They're for *your* wagon if it breaks down,' Hoke said, with a cunning, almost dismissive smirk. 'An' if the same thing happens when we're across the border an' headin' towards the Republican, believe me, there'll be a lot o' folk who won't stop for a busted wagon *then*. Those few more hours'll likely mean the difference between them seein' that dream, or dyin' because of it. Are you prepared to live on that difference?'

They rode on a mile or so in silence, before Peggler spoke.

'I guess you ought to start callin' me Juke,' he said.

'You're payin' me to get you an' these folk to the Plattes, Creek Country. Callin' you Juke don't mean there's a more favourable way o' doin' it.'

Peggler was going to say that it wasn't exactly what he had in mind, but didn't. Whatever he thought of Hoke John's disposition, it was the man's ways and means that would get them to where they were going. Bearing in mind that the journey wouldn't last for ever, he grunted a response.

11

Early next morning the train had hardly stirred before Hoke was calling for a move. It was two hours earlier than previous starts to the day and the ground still held the frostiness of night. Hoke was setting a new pace for the wagon-train's journey towards the Nebraska border. He told Milroy Peggler, the herd drovers and train representatives to urge the cattle and wagons to greater speed.

For many days, Hoke forced a relentless push, even using the morning graze to progress a few more miles. Under the sun for hours on end, the drivers were burning up, their tempers stretched and nerves ragged. In the evenings, quarrels broke out, and more than once, Peggler had to get between whirling fists before Hoke arrived.

Worried about the break-up of morale, Dixie Tennon decided to speak with Peggler about Hoke's new strategy.

'It's like we're all bein' pushed for his sake, Milroy,' he reckoned. 'Speak to him ... find out what's goin' on.'

'I already did, Dixie. He reminded me that we all traded crossin' the Republican with doin' it his way.'

'Some o' the older ones are gettin' tired,' Dixie continued. 'If it was the badlands he was runnin' us through, I'd understand ... but it ain't.'

'I'm sorry, Dixie, but we don't have a special lingerin' pace for the aged. Everyone on this trek's supposed to be able-bodied.' Peggler reached out and gave a reassuring grip to Dixie's shoulder. 'Go an' calm 'em down. Tell 'em Nebraska's full o' health resorts an' goddamn infirmaries.'

The next day, Hoke John persisted with his gruelling advance. Now, more than the train elders were being pushed to the limits of their control. They'd not been able to take any rest, and eaten only what they'd been able to hash up on their moving wagons. Everybody was longing for sleep, and after nearly fifteen hours of driving, there was no exchange of friendly banter that night.

And there was no let up. Long before noon the following day, tired, sullen families were once again being harried into movement. The menfolk had become dangerously troubled, and Hoke could sense the hostile mood as he rode the check line.

It was during late afternoon when, far off the end of the line, Hoke heard the unmistakable shooting of a rifle. He swung his horse's head and dug in his heels, took a fast canter towards the sound.

Someone was systematically pumping bullets into the burrow holes of a gopher township. From the driving seat of a wagon, the man's aim was good, but it was the only thing that impressed Hoke. He reined in his horse and gripped at the front hoop.

'What the hell are you doin', feller?' he yelled. 'Put that goddamn rifle down, or I'll break it over your thick head.'

The man was solidly built, carried big arms and hands. A heavy moustache made him look older than his years. He held the butt of a Winchester against the driving seat, smiled to himself and pointed it towards the sky. Then, cool and composed he turned to face Hoke.

'I'm just lettin' off a bit o' steam, Mr John. If I don't do somethin', I'm likely to put a pattern o' bullets into the son-of-a-bitch who's troublin' this wagon-train,' he replied coolly. The man was close to Hoke, and spirit showed brightly in his eyes. 'Now, unless you got any objections, right here's where I'll be in shake-down 'til sometime tomorrow.'

Hoke took off his Stetson, hung it on the horn of his saddle. 'Well, if I'm the son-of-a-bitch you say I am, you've sure gone the right way to get your fight,' he offered. 'An' it's just about the only goddamn thing I'll stop on the trail for.' With that, Hoke dismounted and removed his gunbelt and Stetson.

Unruffled, the man laid the rifle and his bleached fedora on the seat beside him. Then he climbed down and turned back his sleeves.

'Unless it's lawful business, I guess what a man's called is his own affair,' Hoke said. 'But in your case, I'm kind o' curious.'

'Sam Kluskey,' the man said simply.

The two men circled warily each other, shifted sideways as Hoke had intended. Sam held his hand up against the dipping sun and Hoke moved in, smacked him hard across the mouth.

Sam shook his head and licked a trickle of blood from his split lip. He spat it into the ground, and without looking up, lunged suddenly at Hoke. Both men went sprawling in the dust. Hoke was underneath and at a disadvantage, but he knew this kind of fighting. As they hit the ground, he was already twisting himself away from Sam's weight. He rolled on to one knee and drove a short, hard punch into the side of Sam's ribs. He heard the sharp intake of breath, and he piled in again. Sam's body recoiled, and Hoke backed off three paces.

Sam pushed himself to his feet. His mouth was bloody, and his face was flushed and ferocious.

'I'll understand if you want to call it a day,' Hoke said almost hopefully. 'If you want to get back on your wagon, I'll say nothin' more if you don't.'

But Sam's dander was up, his fuse well lit. He clenched his fists and made another attack that Hoke didn't want or expect. Sam's raking fist caught him above his eye and it snapped his head sideways. He stumbled and another fist buried itself low in his belly. He grunted out a curse with the pain, and as he doubled-up to protect himself, Sam caught him with a jawbone punch. Hoke's legs buckled, and he staggered back against the front wheel of Sam's wagon. He was shocked, and for a few stunned seconds he took shallow breaths, stared at the ground between his feet. When he looked up, he was confused by the blurred silhouette above him. Sam Kiuskey was standing with his back to the sun, glaring down at him.

Hoke reached up a hand and grabbed one of the wheel spokes. He pulled himself to his feet, sniffed and shook his head. 'Well, Mr Kluskey, I suggest again that you ease up on this line o' reasonin',' he said, clasping his chin. 'Why not get back in line?'

'Because I'm stayin' here 'til tomorrow. I just told you.' Sam was feeling satisfied with having sent Hoke to the ground. 'While I'm down here, perhaps I'll build me a campfire,' he said, confidently.

'Reckon I was right about the thickness o' your head.' Hoke spat the words into the soil, then determinedly, he hauled himself up. Without any form of guard, but with his fists bunched, he walked unswervingly at Sam. The man really should have heeded him, and Hoke John had never asked anybody *three* times. Now, he'd decided to finish what he'd started.

Sam covered up, took the first hard blow

and tried to turn away. Another right-hander caught him in the kidneys and he gasped, staggered with the stab of pain. He turned back, immediately took Hoke's fist deep in his stomach. Hoke drew back his hand and quickly hit him in the side of his face, then again, higher near his eye.

Five solid, rapid punches, and Sam's face was suddenly split and bruised. Blood was running into his mouth, then down and under his chin to his throat. His eyes were swollen and half-closed, and his legs weakened beneath him. He was finished, but he didn't go down.

Hoke took a pace back, then he cursed, stood startled when he saw Arno Rice looking at him from behind the back of the wagon. The youngster's callow face showed fear and repugnance for what he'd been watching.

Hoke turned back to Sam Kluskey. 'Drive your goddamn wagon,' he rasped. 'Any more o' this, an' you'll be goin' south ... not north.' Then, from deep inside, an extraordinary feeling gripped him, something he recalled from far off. As Sam Kluskey stood his ground, one side of his face was revealed by long curly hair. For a moment, Hoke saw pale skin, the scarred flesh of an ear lobe.

Hoke threw off the unsettling reverie and called out to Arno, 'There ain't anythin' more to see here, Arno. But when this feller comes to, help him up an' into his wagon. Whatever happens, don't stay here for longer than half an hour, do you hear?'

With his jaw and half his face aching badly, Hoke pulled on his Stetson and buckled on his gunbelt. Then he went to his horse and climbed stiffly into the saddle. It took him twenty minutes to reach a point well ahead of the train and, as he rode, he wondered how much more control he'd lose as soon as Arno Rice put his story about.

After a few minutes, Peggler arrived. He edged his sorrel mare in close and looked across at Hoke. 'You got the look of a man who's been takin' care o' trouble,' he said with a wry grin. 'What the hell does the other feller look like?'

'His name's Sam Kluskey, an' he's wearin' a face like a ploughed-up meadow. Do you know where he's from?' Hoke asked, a shade uneasy.

Peggler shook his head slowly. 'No, he never said. Come to think of it, he never said much at all. An' he don't mix much. If I didn't know any better Hoke, I'd say he was kin o' yours.'

'Hmm. How old do you reckon he is?'

'Strip away some o' them facial whiskers, an' he's probably younger than he looks ... maybe sixteen. He'd only have been havin' a bit o' fun ... wouldn't've meant anythin'. Is there somethin' else?'

'Yeah, I think maybe there is. It's somethin' in his face ... his eyes ... just somethin'.'

'That's tiredness, Hoke. A lot o' these people are plum tuckered. They won't take much more o' your pushin'.'

'Yeah, so I heard. But they'll be takin' it. I've just got to get it through their bear ass

115

heads, that we ain't on some sort o' Sunday School nature trail.'

'Hah. Don't go makin' the mistake o' thinkin' they've all got nothin' much between their ears, Hoke. There's some of 'em chock with learnin', even a school ma'am from Wichita.'

'You reckon *he's* had some school learnin' … Sam Kluskey?' Hoke asked, avoiding the issue, disguising his interest.

'I'd say he had, yeah … some.'

Hoke returned Peggler's enquiring look. 'He was pushin' for a fight: I obliged.'

'An' bein' obligin's one o' your more obligin' qualities,' Peggler retorted.

Hoke twisted in the saddle and immediately winced at the pain in his belly. 'The goin's easy at the moment, Milroy, but it ain't stayin' that way. If someone's goin' to want to fight me every goddamn time I–' Before he finished the sentence, Hoke felt as if he'd been struck by a thunderbolt. Sam Kluskey was Sam Kluskey, *now*. But that wasn't his birth name. That was Samuel

Bannen. The separating years had dramatic-ally changed his appearance and he'd grown. But Hoke knew the young wagon driver he'd beaten to the ground was his son.

'No one's goin' to fight *every* time, Hoke,' Peggler said, interrupting Hoke's confused thoughts. 'You ever thought about commu-nicatin' other than with your fists?'

'I've used a gun once or twice,' Hoke replied dully, his mind suddenly far away. His mind was racing with the extraordinary events that cause a father *and* son to change their names.

Peggler was troubled and worried by Hoke's pigheadedness. 'I ain't goin' up against you,' he said. 'Then I probably ain't goin' to get beat senseless.'

12

Hoke paid little heed to what Milroy Peggler had said, and for another two days he maintained an unrelenting run. When the train struck camp early on the morning of the third day, he decided that all water supplies were going to be conserved, that from then on, each wagon would be eking out a daily ration. The people accepted it because they were all in. They were exhausted, spent from lack of sleep, dried up under countless hours of burning sun.

After five more days of the gruelling trek, Tennon and Lambeth led them to one of the creeks that ran 150 miles south from the Republican River. Everyone had suffered nearly a week of deprivation, now they'd rolled up to as much fresh, free-flowing water as they'd ever want.

An hour after the wagons had pulled in alongside the creek, Milroy Peggler was watching Arno Rice and a few other youngsters hanging for steel-heads from a low cutbank.

'I reckon you knew o' this water,' he suggested to Hoke.

'I know it can run dry overnight,' Hoke answered. 'An' I've seen it so gummy it can swallow cows whole. We're lucky.'

Peggler sat thinking for a moment. 'How long before there's more fresh water?' he asked.

'Five days. Maybe six.'

Peggler, nodded thoughtfully, grinned as he understood Hoke's sanction on the water supplies. 'I was forgettin',' he responded, 'you've been this way before.' He looked along the river-bank to where some folk were collecting brushwood for their cooking fires. 'Those folk would understand if you told 'em *why* you rationed the water.' Hoke didn't answer, and Peggler went on talking. 'Looks like Sam Kluskey's mended,' he said, in good humour. 'He's a lad wrapped in hard bark.'

Hoke turned in the saddle, ran an eye along the line of wagons. 'Yeah,' an' some of it's *inside,*'he agreed. 'You'd think he'd have the savvy to limp a bit.'

'Why? He's no reason to coddle your feelin's. I certainly wouldn't.'

'No I guess not,' Hoke said, his voice suddenly faltering and quiet. 'But if you happen to get the chance, you can tell him he fought real good.'

Peggler shrugged his shoulders. 'An' how am I supposed to know that?' he said. 'I'll just say you were askin' after him. He can take that whichever way he wants.'

Feelings were still running high when the wagons rolled again the following day. On the continuing gruelling journey, prospects became more remote, far-off dreams. The settlers turned to the meantime and how to survive the hostile features of both the land and Hoke John.

In the choking, pungent dust, the vast land

stretched on without end, made a wide circle of the Smoky Hills. Another week, and the many tributary creeks of the Republican had to be forded on the journey north towards the border with Nebraska. When the train arrived parched or drenched at evening camps, the settlers fell asleep to the yapping of ravening coyotes, or the singing of dense, venomous clouds of mosquitoes.

Beneath the stock wagon, the gritty patch-eyed dog pressed its jowls into the parched soil. Hoke saw its eyes reflecting yellow in the glow from the fire and he pitched out a morsel of jerk. 'I bet you never reckoned one day you'd be walkin' to Nebraska,' he said.

Ten days later, the wagon train was noon camped in a green, fertile valley. The soil was good and the land was protected in a great, tree-lined curve of Long Black Lake. The wagon-train's representatives had a meeting with Milroy Peggler and decided they were close to the end of their journey.

'Close enough that we've decided to make

our own separate ways,' Peggler put to Hoke. 'Some of us are more obliged than others, but it don't affect nothin'.'

Hoke pushed his hat back on his head. 'You mean my pay,' he said. 'Have you got it?'

Peggler was surprised at Hoke's terse response, and he shook his head. 'Er, no,' he replied. 'But in a couple o' days I'll be ridin' to Julesburg. There's a cattlemen's bank there. Come with me, an' I'll draw cash.'

Hoke remembered Julesburg from many years ago. It was where he'd gone to trade vegetables for flour and lamp oil, a couple of gewgaws for Coral and young Sam. 'I know the place,' he said. 'Didn't have a bank in them days, though.'

That same evening, while the new settlers enjoyed an improvised, but weary celebration, the two men sat talking beside Peggler's store wagon.

'A dollar says you ain't headed back to Shady Lady,' Peggler said.

'You keep your money,' Hoke replied.

'Like you, I've business to sort out.'

'You ain't in *business,* Hoke. Not that sort, anyway,' Peggler said, and handed over a tin mug that held an inch of brandy that he'd tapped from a small oak barrel. 'I always thought you'd taken up the wagon-master's job 'cause it gave you a purpose for comin' back.'

'Yeah, I did, Milroy. Now I'm here, maybe I'll stake out some land, an' settle down. We'll all be one big happy family.' Hoke drained his mug, got to his feet. 'Thanks for settlin' the trail dust,' he said.

Peggler eyed Hoke warily. 'I don't know what your trouble was back then, Hoke, but remember that times have changed. There's a new social order rolled in. Now, there's government offices to approve an' sanction,' he advised.

Hoke tossed his empty mug at Peggler. 'Only for them who believe in gettin' things approved,' he said with the bite of recollection.

On returning to Creek Country, Hoke John's life seemed to have gone full circle. It seemed fate had taken a hand, and he was facing up to his years of wretchedness. But, if there was any such thing as safety in numbers, perhaps he wouldn't have to fight cowmen from his land, again. Perhaps he *could* start over.

After ten years though, the pain of Red Willow Creek still chewed at his vitals. He was never going to forget those who'd taken the life of his wife and forced him from his land, and he wasn't going to ride away from his son a second time. He pondered on his son's new adopted name of Sam Kluskey. Samuel had retained his christened name, but he'd taken his last from the good Irish folk who'd taken him in, given him schooling.

After their recent fist fight, Hoke wondered if Sam had sensed anything. He'd wanted to explain, let Sam know he was his father. But he knew he could never find the words, make any compensation for the lost years. There was little doubt of the loathing that

Sam would have held for him. He'd be the father who'd deserted him as a child; the man who was to blame for the death of his mother. As such, Sam would have severed Hoke and the name of Bannen from his life.

There was *one* occasion, when Hoke had spoken to Sam. He'd tried to tell him there was no ill-feeling from their ridiculous brawl, even considered offering up a clue to their relationship. But there was no give and take. Sam had listened to Hoke in indifferent silence, then turned away to his new life with the settlers from Kansas.

In due time, and a few miles upriver from the main settlement, Hoke took Peggler's advice, and staked out a small piece of land. With money earned from bringing the wagons in safely, he employed a few men to build him a modest lodging and outbuildings.

Using the Overland Mail out of Julesburg, then telegraph between Kearney and Lincoln, Milroy Peggler engaged land and property agents to sell his interests in Shady

Lady Springs. He would attempt to carve out new business ventures, try again for the elusive fortune.

13

At the southern end of the settlement, an ancient live oak presided over one of the willow brakes that bordered the creeks. It was an obvious landmark and, as such, gave its name to the new township.

The settlers worked hard from the moment they arrived in Creek Country. They yolked mules and ploughed the first furrows, enthusiastically sowed wheat, maize and vegetables. As the months passed, the town of Old Oak grew. They built rough-planked buildings, walled them with canvas and erected false fronts. Then, some merchants added another storey, others put up awnings and built raised sidewalks.

Corn-chandlers, carpenters, livery men and waggoners, even a barber rekindled their trades. Milroy Peggler opened a livery stable and a store that stocked everything from farm machinery and guns, to canned peaches and ladies' bonnets. He also built his saloon and named it Oak's Swallow. In the third year, a telegraph operator opened an office, and a regular mail service was in operation. The Central Pacific drove a rail loop from Grand Island to Sterling, gave the town a trade link that stretched from Chicago in the east to Sacramento and San Francisco in the west.

In a few years, Old Oak grew rapidly in both size and prosperity. In the rich Nebraska soil, the crop yield was choice and abundant. From a breed stock of Poll Durhams, small herds of quality cattle grazed the pasture land that was irrigated by creek water that fingered north from the Republican River. The original immigrant community had grown from nearly 100 to nearly 400.

But like all the emerging, prosperous towns of the North Central United States, it was considered a turkey shoot for gunmen, gamblers and hell-raisers. Saloon girls and faro tables vied to separate the townsfolk from their hard-earned money, and a black-smith and a doctor strived to repair the breakages. At one end of town, a bank and a stage office operated during daylight hours. At the other end, a small tented city supplied cheap liquor to farmers and trail drifters as soon as the sun dropped. The resulting gun play even created trade for the undertaker, who'd claim civic payment for digging and filling another hole in Old Oak's boneyard.

The few original spokesmen who'd got together in Shady Lady Springs when the settlers decided to set out, still held regular meetings. Milroy Peggler was one of them, and one of the first to realize the trouble that was emerging. The unavoidable scourge of lawlessness, forced the spokesmen to create a recognized town council. Their first remit was to seek and nominate a reliable and determined man for sheriff.

Sam Kluskey found the job rewarding, but it

was an arduous task. He deputized Dixie Tennon and Jack Lambeth to curb disorderly conduct and keep gunfighting off the streets. With his own zeal and frequent employment of gun barrel and fists, law and order was steadily enforced. For Sam Kluskey, the dispensing of makeshift justice came as second nature, like an inherited feature. As a fair-minded officer, he'd back off from any fair fight, but deal harshly with wilful, unjust killing, mob rule or horse-thieving.

As time passed and the law established itself, Old Oak began to attract a different sort of trouble. Corrupt speculators and finance cheats were attracted by the thriving community, the opportunity for quick and easy profits. Businesses that were once carried out by robbery and intimidation, were now implemented by fraud and deception within the small print.

During this time, Hoke partook of a peaceable, almost reclusive life, and his needs were modest. He appeared to be content with tending his tract of land, and the occasional game of cards in Oak's Swallow. But only Hoke knew it was a cover for what he was really doing. He was close to Sam Kluskey, living out a lot of his own wanting life through his son's. Seeing Sam carry out his duties of sheriff gave him an almost visceral pleasure, cured some of the hurt he'd felt since the death of his wife.

But, after the horrors of Red Willow Creek, the life of a farmer meant very little to Hoke. At a time and place where reputations only lasted as long as it took to get measured for a pine box, very few people knew about the reasons behind Hoke's return. Once in a while, Hoke would talk with Milroy Peggler, manoeuvre the conversation round to the sheriff and his activities. He saw Sam, but he never spoke. Sam would nod to him from his office across the street, but it was a passing, stiff recognition, nothing more. Hoke thought it must be more than their fist fight that created the wall between them. His private ordeal was something he'd never felt the like of.

14

One late fall evening, Hoke was sitting on the sidewalk outside of Oak's Swallow. He was pondering on the day, when a man wearing a heavy twill suit stepped up alongside his seat. Hoke didn't look up, but he'd kept the man in his peripheral vision.

'I didn't recognize you from across the street,' the man said. 'But now I can see it's you ... underneath them whiskers, that is. Name's Bannen ... once farmed dirt along Red Willow Creek.'

Suddenly, Hoke realized the day was gaining some chill, and it made him shiver. 'Are you askin' or tellin', feller?' he responded, quietly.

'I guess I'm tellin',' the man said evenly. 'I ain't gone for the changes you have, Bannen, so it should be easier for you to remember.'

Hoke considered whether to look up. He thought about his gun back at the cabin, then he turned his head. 'I'm reachin' a time in my life when I'm castin' out a lot o' remembered stuff. No gain in it,' he drawled. 'But in your case I'll make an exception,' he told the man.

The man was nervy, and Hoke knew why he should be. He was Otis Pipe, the man whom Coral had stopped him from kicking to death alongside Red Willow Creek. Pipe's last rasping words were to tell them both there'd be a price to pay.

And there was. It was Ramsay Polman and the Three Creeks riders. They came back to burn his home and had killed Coral. Now, Hoke stared hard at the man he'd near whipped to death. His gut knotted as he remembered the look on Owen Pipe's face as the man's knife tore at young Sam's ear.

Pipe looked up and down the street. 'Before you do somethin' you'll regret, Bannen, or whatever you call yourself, I got somethin' to say,' he said. 'But *you'll* need a drink ... an' I'll likely need witnesses.'

'Courtesy o' my wife, you've had about fifteen years' livin', Pipe. So, if you think I'm goin' to worry about *witnesses,* you still got real trouble,' Hoke answered, his eyes fixed and icy. 'I ain't about to regret nothin', not even if the whole town's out front an' watchin' from pay chairs.'

Hoke was grinding on his thoughts and feelings as he got to his feet. Within moments, fifteen years didn't seem like such a long time ago.

Pipe shrugged, and as he pushed his way through the doors of the saloon, Hoke clenched his fists. He followed Pipe to the bar, threw a measured glance around him.

'I don't know what the hell you're up to, Pipe,' he hissed. 'Give me a reason why I don't rip your black heart out right now.'

Pipe thought for a second. 'I'll give you two,' he answered. 'The fact you got to ask, an' the law.'

Pipe grabbed at the bottle the bartender pushed across the counter. He poured into one of two glasses. 'I said I'd hound you for the rest of my life for killin' Owen,' he said. He looked at Hoke, swallowed the whiskey in a single gulp.

Hoke's heart was thumping and his temper was cracking. 'Your brother was a gutless life form an' needed destroyin'. An' as for the rest o' *your* life, that suddenly ain't too far off,' he rasped.

'Time ain't cramped that temper o' yours, Bannen,' Pipe retorted. 'There's some say it's what caused most o' your trouble. Well, I've got some-thin' to say on another score.'

'Yeah? Is that what you need them witnesses for ... when you do it?'

Pipe disregarded Hoke's glass and poured himself another whiskey. 'I'm here to tell you, Bannen ... or whoever you are ... that you really should've bought that strip o' land you reckon you own.'

'How'd you find me, Pipe? What the hell are you doin' here?' Hoke was squeezing an empty glass, the knuckles of his big fingers hard-stretched and white. He breathed heavy as Pipe told him.

A year previous, after wearying of cattle life, Otis Pipe had chance-met Jump Geigan and Arkie Munce in Shady Lady Springs. Munce told him that he'd seen Hoke Bannen, that the man who'd killed his brother had taken a wagon-train to the Creek Country many years before. Now, fifteen years on he'd caught up with the man who was calling himself Hoke John. But the days of rough, summary justice were drawing to a chose, and Otis Pipe had to find another way to exact his festered retribution.

Hoke glared at him. 'Christ, Pipe, you got to be the most stupid, dumb animal ever to tread soil. After all these years, you're goin' to make an issue o' my land ... again?' Hoke's jaw twitched and he slammed the glass hard against the counter.

Some of Pipe's assurance drained away as he recalled the force of the tough farmer's temper, and one or two customers edged away from the bar. He was troubled now, gave a lean smirk as he tentatively pulled a folded piece of paper from an inside pocket. 'This is a deed, Bannen,' he explained carefully. 'The title's on the piece o' land you're sittin' on.'

Hoke ground his teeth, and made a grab for the document.

'Perhaps I should've said, it's a copy. The original's filed in Julesburg,' Pipe said, flinching back a pace. 'You can set fire to it or eat it, it don't matter much.'

Hoke opened up the single sheet of paper and carefully read the words. With crawling unease, he tried to understand the legal jargon. With the anguish showing on his face, he looked at Pipe. 'Where'd you get this?' he challenged.

'Where an' how don't matter, but your land does belong to me. Has done for a long week.'

Hoke laughed nervously. 'I can see you ain't given this much thought, mister,' he offered. 'You ain't workin' any land when all you got is stump knees to get around on.'

Pipe shook his head. 'Threats won't win

you this one, Bannen. I got every territory, state an' federal conveyancin' act on my side. Soon, I'll be returnin' to Julesburg to get an order for the land to be cleared, an' you along with it. So think about my proposition before I leave.'

'What hell proposition? You just been tellin' me there ain't one,' Hoke scowled, strung out with anger.

'I'm proposin' you buy me out. It's a good deal for good land. If you're happy there, make me a good offer.'

It was then that the truth of what was happening got to Hoke. 'I understand,' he said, and slowly released the whiskey glass. He shook his head cheerlessly. 'I'm bearin' in mind the law enforcement o' this town, Pipe. So, before I either kill or pay you, I'm gettin' someone to look at these shyster words,' he threatened.

Before Pipe could respond, Hoke's hand snapped up around his neck. The pain was instant as Hoke's fingers crushed into his throat. He wilted, his arms and legs hung limp as his feet left the ground and his bulging eyes came close to Hoke's enraged face.

'Not killin' *you* always was a big regret,' Hoke rasped. 'It's been a cancer festerin' away inside me.' Then he let go of Pipe's neck and snatched up the deed. He grabbed at the man's coat and dragged him across the room, slammed his head hard through the batwings.

15

Otis Pipe stumbled on to the sidewalk and Hoke kicked him straight into the dirt of the street. The small number of saloon customers were sensible enough to stay back, but the commotion attracted the attention of a few passers-by.

Since Sam Kluskey had taken a grip on the town, street brawling was a rarer form of Old Oak's entertainment. But this was obviously a one-sided affair, and more than a fist or gunfight. The folk watched as Hoke crossed the road, guffawed with interest as he manhandled Pipe along to the double-fronted hardware store.

From behind his big utilitarian desk at the rear of his store, Milroy Peggler looked up startled as the door crashed open. He pulled off his pince-nez and got to his feet. 'Hoke?

What the hell are–?' he began, then swore as Hoke swung Pipe roughly up against a row of his stock shelves.

'You know somethin' of legal papers, Milroy. Tell me about this.' Hoke held Pipe's deed paper out to Peggler. 'What's it mean?' he said.

Pipe thought there might be some protection in Peggler's presence and the validity of his deed. 'If you know anythin', tell this Bannen feller, or whatever the hell his name is, it's legal,' he yelled his resentment. 'Tell him *that.*'

But Peggler was more interested in something other than Pipe's blustering. As he read the piece of paper, he picked up on the name, Bannen. All of a sudden he was thinking back to Shady Lady Springs and Hoke's interest in Arkie Munce, the one-armed gambler.

'I hope you know what you're doin', Pipe,' Hoke threatened. 'If you've ever come by any family, think o' them.'

Pipe assessed the hostile atmosphere, saw

the harm in pushing Hoke any further as he rubbed at the ache in his neck.

Peggler looked up, sniffed and let the document drop to his desk. He took a long hard look at Pipe. 'I was often tellin' Mr John to get a legal claim fitted to his land, but I must admit I always thought it would be in the interests of resale, not to stop some low-life embezzler takin' it from him,' he said. 'An' *this* is Otis Pipe, is it?' he asked, turning to Hoke.

'Oh yeah, no doubtin' that. An' he'll be carryin' some scars to prove it.' Hoke looked uneasily from Peggler to Pipe, back to Peggler. 'You knew I weren't ever goin' to bother registerin' that land, Milroy. With more land than anyone's ever seen in their life, who'd want to bother with my handker-chief plot? What the hell's goin' on?' he added, hesitantly.

Feeling for a cigar, Peggler patted his top pocket. 'This document's a copy, Hoke, but that don't make it illegal. Otis Pipe appears to be the legal owner of a piece o' land that must be real special,' he intimated thought-fully. 'Why, an' what's goin' on, I really don't know. But I reckon you do.' Hoke stood very still taking deep breaths. Pipe was staring at Peggler, nodding with expectation. Peggler shook his head. 'Are you goin' to tell me?' he asked of Hoke.

While Hoke made an effort to deal with his confused thoughts, Peggler briefly ex-plained how Pipe obtained the land deed.

'Washington made an enactment for settlers, whereby anyone could stake out a section of land. All they had to do was make a register, an' it was theirs, watertight, legal an' for evermore.' Peggler drew out his cigar. 'You knew *that*, Hoke, but Mr Pipe here must've poked around some filin' cabinets out at Julesburg. You've been euchred an' it's personal ... real close. Why is that, Hoke? Tell me, an' I'll be the wiser.'

'I shot his brother,' Hoke said tersely. 'They were runnin' me off my land. They caught my boy an' mutilated him. He weren't into double years an' they crop-eared him. An' it was Pipe's outfit that killed my wife. It was a long time ago, but not that long.'

Peggler toyed with the cigar, rolled it between his fingers. 'I guessed it was somethin' but not–' he was saying, when the penny dropped. 'Goddamnit, Hoke, it was up here,' he realized. 'That's how you knew the Creek Country. It's why you brought the wagon-train,' he said, putting it together. 'You had to come back.'

Hoke had turned away, was looking out the dusty, glass-paned door. A blue norther was riffling the street dirt, and within a few days, the first snow would roll north from the Smokies. It would get cold, and icy winds would seek out every nook and cranny in all of the Old Oak buildings.

Peggler bit off the end of his cigar, spat it into the floor. 'You're wretched trash, mister,' he levelled at Pipe. 'I'm a simple trader who sells stuff for small profits an' gets to read the occasional document. So, if you think you're safe here, forget it. I don't do protection. You're goin' to need the

144

sheriff's office.'

Hoke was still looking out the door, but he heard what Peggler had said. He cursed inwardly, was thinking how things would transpire if Sam knew the identity of Pipe. 'I wouldn't go there,' he advised, keeping any significance from his voice. 'What should I be doin', Milroy?' he asked.

'What would Hoke Bannen have done twenty years ago?' Peggler answered.

Pipe was edging along the shelves, his eyes flickering with fear. 'I'm offerin' to sell it to you for a fair price, Bannen. I ain't done nothin' illegal,' he uttered.

Hoke's insides churned with rage. 'You're still breathin',' he snarled, balling his fist and moving at Pipe.

Pipe shifted quickly behind Peggler's desk, but Peggler thrust out an arm. 'No!' he shouted, and turned towards Hoke, flattened a hand against his chest 'Think about it, Hoke. It's an act o' vengeance. He wants somethin' to settle the score for his brother. I know it's very stupid, the reasonin' of a lame brain, but go with it. What's your land worth?'

Hoke didn't answer, just stared silently at Pipe.

'Think,' Peggler continued. 'This louse reckons it's worth the life of his brother.'

'He was a spineless coward,' Hoke said, his intention unreadable. 'My land's suddenly worth everythin'; his brother was worth...' Hoke appeared to smile before he finished what he was saying. He bent down to grab at something on the floor, then stood up and took a pace slowly towards Pipe. He raised his hand and slammed it hard across Pipe's mouth, up into his nose. 'Boot muck an' plug spit. That's the worth of you an' your brother,' he rasped. 'Now get out. Get out o' Nebraska before I kill you.'

Peggler stepped forward and clutched at the lapels of Pipe's coat. He opened the door, and shoved him on to the sidewalk. 'No one can be this stupid, mister. Get away from here, before my friend decides to settle up,' he snapped.

For the second time, Otis Pipe had seen death in the man he knew as Hoke Bannen. He was scared, and ten minutes later he was locked in his room in the run-down boarding-house at the south end of town. Still wanting revenge, he knew he'd try again and his trembling worsened.

Standing outside of Peggler's store, Hoke too was shaking. But it wasn't from fear. 'I should've done more,' he muttered, at the thought of starting over with Pipe's retribution.

16

Muffled in a long beaver coat, Hoke John was sitting in an old chair on the stoop of his weather-boarded cabin. The trees that edged the creeks of the Republican River were brightly rimed with frost, and the year's first snow carpeted the land. It was too cold for the ancient dog that was inside, curled asleep on Hoke's straw-filled pallet.

Hoke felt a chill river of sweat run down his neck. He shivered when he saw the rig approaching along the crisp white ridges of the wagon road. 'Looks like you or me's got 'emselves a visitor,' he muttered.

Whoever it was, had a muffler wrapped tight around their hat, but Hoke already knew it to be Miles Esham.

The owner of the boarding-house pulled one hand from a fur glove. He'd ridden five miles, but Hoke's welcoming wasn't running to coffee anymore. Esham seemed to know it, had the rig half turned, before he held out a folded envelope.

Hoke pushed himself from his chair and stretched out a hand.

'I was paid to bring it,' Esham said, indifferently.

Hoke nodded. 'I wouldn't want to think you did it as a favour,' he replied. He took the envelope and looked hard at the writing. HOKE JOHN – FORMERLY HOKE BANNEN, it said. 'Who sent me this?' he shouted.

'No matter, there ain't no answer,' Esham yelled back. Then he flicked the reins, was off at a trot, back to Old Oak.

The dog was wakened by the voices and yowled his pique from inside the cabin.

'I'll be in when I've read this,' Hoke responded testily. He stood by the door, smoothed out the envelope with his forefinger and thumb. He pulled out the single sheet of paper and ran his eyes over the page. Then he looked south towards the Kansas border and the Smoky Hills. A muscle twitched beneath his eye, and he crumpled up the paper.

The letter was notification from a lawyer in Julesburg, and the gist of it was clear. If Hoke didn't quit his land, a judgment would be made against him. If he didn't comply, an authorized force would be despatched to forcibly escort him off the property. However, the judgment would be withdrawn, if payment of $1,000 was deposited at the Fullway Bank in Julesburg. Hoke had forty-eight hours to raise the money, to buy his own land from Otis Pipe.

For a long time Hoke stared out into the brilliant, crystal clear air. At nearly a mile, he wondered if he could hit the messenger with a Winchester bullet. 'I did warn Pipe. An' it ain't goin' to take me two days to pay,' he said. His voice was subdued, and forbidding.

The dog opened a watchful eye, knew not to make much of a fuss when Hoke stepped into the relative warmth of the cabin. Hoke took a jug from the stove, and poured himself a mug of coffee. Then he pulled a small wooden chest from the far side of his pallet. Inside was a gunbelt and a waxed cardboard box containing ammunition. Wrapped in an oily cloth was his old .44 Colt and a spare cylinder. 'You learn there's some folk make you think an' do things that you'd rather live without, goddamnit,' he said, and looked at the dog for a moment.

When Hoke rode into town later that day, there were one or two bystanders who eyed him with curiosity. There were still a few settlers who recalled the disposition of wagonmaster Hoke Bannen. Those who felt an unease similar to when they'd set out from Shady Lady Springs, nearly six years ago.

Hoke went straight to Milroy Peggler and showed him the letter. With muddled reasoning, Hoke regarded Peggler's office as the law. To him, the sheriff's office was forbidden, stranger territory.

'They got you cold-cocked, Hoke. This Otis Pipe means business, an' he's got the law on his side.' Peggler sensed the potential danger when he saw Hoke wearing his gun. 'I know you only ever wanted to be an honest man, Hoke,' he said. 'Some day there'll be laws to protect honest folk, instead of displacin' 'em.'

'Yeah. Meanwhile my land gets stolen by Pipe an' his 'breed. Well I ain't bein' displaced, Milroy. Until that "some day" gets here, I'm usin' my law.'

'You know we're tryin' to do things right in Old Oak,' Peggler said seriously. He held up his hand as he anticipated Hoke's interruption. 'Why can't you go to Sam Kluskey? Is there some reason? Somethin' else you ain't ever told me?'

For a moment, Hoke looked hard at Peggler. 'If the sheriff only knew, he'd back me against Otis Pipe.'

'If he only knew *what*, Hoke?'

'If he *knew* it was Otis Pipe an' his brother who gave him that chewed-up ear.'

'Christ! *Pipe* did that to Sam's ear?' Peggler asked incredulously.

'He held him. His brother, Owen, did the cuttin'. Sam Kluskey's pa killed him for it. That's what it is with Pipe. He wants to take everythin' from me.'

'I don't understand. Why would Pipe want to take land from *you*, Hoke?'

'It was *me* did the killin': I'm Sam Kluskey's pa.'

'I should've guessed,' he said. 'Those years back, when you wanted him to know he fought you good. You wanted me to tell him, remember?'

Hoke nodded silently.

'An' you've avoided your own son for five years.' Peggler said, and shook his head with obvious feeling. 'Leave the goddamn land, Hoke,' he then added, but with fervour. 'Let him sell to someone else, or give it away. Make your peace with Sam. I'll loan you the money to build another home. An' have some o' my land. What the hell do I need it for? Fifty yards past tent city, an' I'm feelin' homesick. Just think about it. It ain't too late.'

'It is for Otis Pipe. I thank you for the offer, Milroy, but after Red Willow Creek, I vowed nobody would ever move me on again.'

'You're more'n pig-headed, Hoke. You're willin' to lose–' But Peggler didn't bother to say any more, because the bell above the door had already pinged as the door closed. His thoughts were running similar to those of Ramsay Polman, fifteen years earlier. Soon, someone was going to suffer at the hands of Hoke John.

17

Two days later, Hoke was out front of his cabin, chopping logs. Big flakes of snow were falling and the land was smothered in a bright, peaceful hush. It was only when Hoke stopped for a moment to draw breath, that he heard the unmistakable jingle of a spur. The cold was biting deep into the old dog's bones now, and he rarely emerged from the cabin. He didn't bother much about sounds, other than meat slapping on to a tin plate.

Sam Kluskey was coming down the wagon road. His horse was walking, occasionally shying at the soft footing. When he was thirty yards from the cabin he dismounted, tied in the horse to a bankside willow. He drew a carbine from a saddle holster, angled it over his shoulder.

Hoke swung the axe, drove its blade deep

into a wood block. Normally he would have gone for the Winchester, but he was hoping he wouldn't need it for the sheriff of Old Oak.

A dozen paces off, Sam stopped. 'You know why I'm here, Mr John,' he called.

'Yeah, reckon I do, Sheriff.'

'I have to serve the notice. It comes with the job, nothin' personal.' Adjusting his carbine, he pulled a sheet of paper from inside his heavy mackinaw. 'It's an eviction order. But, you'd've known it was comin' if you'd read the summons. You want to take a look at it?' he asked.

'No.' Hoke squeezed haft of his axe with frustration. He wanted to ask Sam if he'd do the same thing if he knew it *was* personal.

'The time's up ... you had forty-eight hours. I'll be back tomorrow ... give you another day.'

Hoke shook with emotion. He hardly knew what to say, how to respond. The sheriff telling him to move on, was his own son. 'I ain't leavin',' he said slowly. 'Folk shouldn't be pushed from the land that's rightly theirs. There's got to be an end to it.' Hoke waved an arm around him. 'You know this is my land, Sheriff. I'm ready to die for it, if I have to.'

'That's just about what I been told, Mr John. But I'm sworn to uphold the law, not to take people's lives. If they decide otherwise, then I'll do that as well, if I have to.'

'Yeah, an' that's just about what I know of you, Sheriff. You're supportin' a law that makes it legal to rob me of everythin'. So maybe you'll be killin' me tomorrow.'

Sam's face hardly moved. 'Maybe?' he asked quizzically.

'Well, I ain't gain' to stand here, wincin' as the bullets hit, Sheriff Kluskey.'

Sam thought for a few moments. He was oddly moved by Hoke's reaction, his stubbornness. 'I'll be here, noon tomorrow,' he said inevitably.

Hoke swallowed hard against the lump in his throat; for twenty minutes, watched after Sam Kluskey. He lost sight of him after ten, but disturbed, rising crows plotted his course back along the creek. For the remainder of the day he swung the axe, then through the night he lay on his pallet, deep in thought. He didn't bother to rekindle the stove, so he shivered. He was suffering from the clash of emotions that beset him, his enmity of Otis Pipe and being forced off his land. But that wasn't going to happen again, and that's what really worried him. How would he fare against Sam and his badge of office?

The dog was tugging at his trousers when the mighty Nebraska sky broke into dawn. The snow was deep and had drifted against the front of his cabin. The silence was total, almost painful. He fed the dog some pone and hogjaw, spent the next few hours staring at the underside of his roof. Between the bank of the river and Hoke's cabin, three horsemen pulled up. Without speaking one of them dismounted and ground-hitched his horse. Dixie Pennon and Jack Lambeth wore overcoats, had their hat brims folded down across their ears and tied under their chins. Sam Kluskey was wearing his long, plaid mackinaw.

The dog raised an eye, an ear barely flicked. 'Yeah, I know, I've been waitin' for 'em,' Hoke muttered and stared at the Winchester. 'An' I'm plumb out of options.' He lifted the latch and pulled the door open. A drifted wedge of snow crumpled at his feet, and the cold air smacked hard against him.

Beside the small rope corral, Sam Kluskey was holding his carbine, the barrel pointing into the thick snow. Through the frosty breath that clouded his face, his eyes were set on Hoke.

Hoke's Winchester was loaded, but there was no way he'd lever a shell into the breech, let alone pull the trigger. He wondered if Sam had noticed that. He thought of shouting, telling Sam Kluskey, that to *him*, he'd always be Samuel Bannen.

Slowly but surely, Sam advanced and Hoke knew the confrontation was over. For all the good it was going to do him, he wondered why he hadn't left his gun in the cabin.

Sam stepped up to within a dozen paces of Hoke. The merest trace of a smile crossed his face, then surprise. 'I reckon if you were going to make a fight of it, Mr John, you'd have used that Winchester from the window,' he suggested.

'Pretty sure o' yourself, aren't you, Son?' Hoke returned the thin smile, considering the standpoint, thought his choice of words mildly amusing.

'More sure o' you,' Sam replied. 'Ill fares the land in which money is more than men, Mr John. I thought you'd know that.'

Hoke knew it very well, and the last time that he'd stood in front of his cabin with a loaded gun, there'd been three Bannens. Now, his wife was dead, and his son was both a full-grown stranger and a town sheriff.

Hoke didn't try to understand, didn't answer. He just stared uncertainly at Sam, felt the emptiness in the pit of his stomach. He thought how easy it would be if he made a sudden move, if he brought up his gun. He wondered how long it would take Tennon and Lambeth to put bullets into him, whether Sam would join in.

'Let go o' the gun, Mr John. You know what we're here for ... what you have to do,' Sam said, not entirely without feeling.

Still, Hoke said nothing, and it worried Sam.

'Drop the rifle, Mr John,' he repeated. 'We can talk ... discuss it some.'

'Huh, you'd be mighty surprised at any talkin' I got to do, Sheriff. Here take it,' Hoke said, resignedly, and held out the Winchester.

Sam took the gun, looked back at Hoke. 'Must be about six years since we got so close. You ain't figurin' on takin' back your gun, are you, Mr John?'

'No, not while you got two deputies workin' for you.'

Sam looked back at Tennon and Lambeth. 'Yeah. Like me, they're paid to support the law,' he said.

Hoke reached inside the cabin door, pulled a rolled blanket and slicker from a peg. Without another word, he walked down the steps and strode past Sam towards the corral. 'If your boys are goin' in there to housemaid for Mr Pipe, tell 'em to look out for the dog. It won't move, so they'll probably have to shoot it,' he called out, bitterly.

Hoke tugged at the door of a lean-to stall. It took him five minutes to saddle his mare, then he rode away without looking back.

Tennon and Lambeth had rode closer to the cabin, but Sam Kluskey hadn't moved inside. All three men watched silently as Hoke vanished under the falling blanket of snow.

'He don't deserve that,' Sam said to Lambeth.

'No, an' we don't deserve to be froze up out here. But we done our job, Sam. The man's beat, an' he won't be back,' Carrow replied.

'Wrong.' Sam's voice was almost a whisper. 'You're wrong on both counts. He ain't beat, an' he will be back. He knows it, an' I know it.'

18

Dixie Tennon didn't waste much time in spreading the word how the law had faced down Hoke John, the tyrant of the wagon-train from Shady Lady Springs. Quickly, the story spread throughout the town and the creeks.

Sam Kluskey hadn't said anything, it wasn't his way. But he heard the gossip about the man who had once been notorious for his belligerence and fighting ability, surrendering his gun. Evidently, Hoke John had turned his back on his home, rode off without so much as a shaken fist.

There was no one, not even Milroy Peggler who knew of Hoke's whereabouts, where he'd likely be headed. No one seemed that bothered, except the sheriff. At that time of the year, and with no weather break, Sam

Kluskey knew you didn't go far with only a bedroll for comfort.

It was five days later when Hoke reappeared. When he walked into the Oak's Swallow Saloon his eyes were sunken, and with his huddled, distressed appearance he went unrecognized. When he moved quietly to the bar and ordered a schooner of beer, no one noticed the .44 Colt tucked inside his jacket.

Hoke kept his head down, listened to the local talk. There was some excitement and some crude jokes, all of it centred around Miss Penny Pinches.

Penny Pinches was actually Penelope Bud, a touring cantatrice, whom Milroy Peggler had engaged to perform at Oak's Swallow. But, like half-a-dozen other visitors and passers-through, she'd been delayed because of deep snow between Old Oak and the rail-head at Julesburg. She was famed through-out the reach of the Central Pacific Rail Road, allegedly gained her 'stage name' from the way she handled the amorous advances of drunken cowboys.

Milroy Peggler reckoned he was in for a handsome profit. The cost of just one Penny Pinches performance ticket was nearly as much as most folk earned in a week. But enough of them had dug deep, and Peggler was looking to cram in a few more lucrative performances.

Although Penny was the object of much interest and animated vulgarity, not everyone in Old Oak was joining in. As Hoke stood at the bar, wrapped in his more ill-fated thoughts, he started at a voice close beside him.

'I don't reckon he's ever goin' to turn up here,' a man proclaimed. 'He's a dog that's had his day. Otis waves his bit o' paper, says "boo", an' he just hands him his land. Sheriff tells him to get packed an' he slinks off into the snow. No, I don't reckon that ol' tomato kisser will cast a shadow here again.'

Hoke stared hard at the beer ring on the counter in front of him. He tried to remember, tried to place the insult and the man's voice.

The man loudly demanded another whiskey. 'But you be sure to let me know if you do see him. I'll be stickin' around 'til this goddamn snow clears,' he said. Then he tossed back his whiskey and walked towards the swing doors.

But the memory of a violent and painful brawl had come back to Hoke. 'Hey, mister,' he grated, 'was it one o' them tomato kissers who made such a mess o' your face?'

It was the edge to Hoke's voice that sent a hush across the room. That, and because a few of the customers suddenly realized it was Hoke John, standing at the bar.

Hoke stood upright, took a small sideways step as he addressed the back of the stranger. Halfway to the swing doors, the man stopped and turned slowly. He gave a long, penetrating look at Hoke. 'You,' he said simply.

It was Jump Geigan, one of those who'd run cattle along Red Willow Creek. After the fight with Hoke, he'd moved on from Tapps Morgan's outfit, made himself a small reputation by fleecing settlers and landbreakers along the North Platte. Later, having to contend with increasing law and order, he'd drifted south into Kansas, met up with Arkie Munce and Otis Pipe in Shady Lady Springs. It was there they'd talked about the man now known as Hoke John.

After ten, twelve years, the two men hardly recognized each other. Geigan was heavier than he had been, but still carried the scars on his face and the shattered nose from Hoke's beating.

Hoke looked calm, but his nerves were jangling. He could hardly believe it. Were they all back to get him? After what he'd done to them all those years before, were they all coming back for revenge? No one had paid a higher price than Hoke for what had happened then, and time *had* taken its toll. Hoke was tired of fighting for a lone, peaceable life, and the thought of a return match with Jump Geigan hadn't crossed his mind. But that didn't mean it was dead and buried.

Geigan had been surprised though, it wasn't the way he'd planned the reunion. His gut churned and he felt a tightening of the scar tissue across his disfigured race. He saw immediately that Hoke didn't appear to carry a gun, wondered if perhaps the man he'd known as Hoke Bannen had been run off his land, finally a beaten man.

Jump Geigan had lost any advantage of taking Hoke unawares, and he felt sweat break across his scalp. He looked Hoke up and down. 'Don't look like you're up to handin' out punishment any more,' he managed without much faith. 'More like takin' hand-outs,' he added foolishly.

The customers standing near to the bar backed off, and others cleared a space between the two men. Hoke was aware that most eyes in the saloon were on him. It was too early in the day for Milroy Peggler to be around, not even tending paperwork in the small annexed office.

'You said somethin' like that once before,

Geigan,' Hoke snarled. An' it was a mistake *then.*'

A vengeful smirk warped Geigan's mouth. He stepped forward a pace, his stance challenging. 'That was *then*. Now it's my time,' he snapped back.

Hoke seemed to sigh, but his eyes bore deep into Geigan. 'Well, get on with it, you ugly son-of-a-bitch,' he said. 'Or do you want I should flannel you like I did last time?'

Inside the saloon, the stillness and silence was total when Hoke slowly pulled the big Colt from his jacket. Without taking his eyes off Geigan he set the action and placed it carefully on the bar counter beside him. He nodded imperceptibly at his adversary.

Geigan swallowed hard. With his right hand he pulled aside the flap of his range coat, revealed a Starr revolver holstered loose around his waist. As he felt his boldness seep away, he thought that maybe Hoke was full of bluff, maybe the big Colt was too high on the counter, maybe the farmer from Red Willow Creek was a tomato kisser when it came to gun play. Yeah, maybe, he thought as went for his gun.

For a man going to fat, Geigan was quick. He managed to get his hand around the bone-handled butt before Hoke's first bullet hit him high in the chest. The horror of pain didn't get to him until the second shot blew his neck apart. As he staggered backwards, he saw a cluster of ceiling lamps whirl around as he fell, tasted the blood as it filled his mouth. Before death brought on the crushing blackness, he even had time to consider the mistake he'd made.

As the gunshots crashed and reverberated, Hoke fired again. Twice more he hit Geigan, watched coldly as the big bullets slammed home. 'That's it,' he said, 'there won't be a third time.'

19

Through the hanging gunsmoke and acrid bite of powder, the clients of Oak's Swallow stared at Hoke, then at the body of Geigan. Hoke put his gun back on the counter and motioned to the bartender. 'Make it a whiskey ... Milroy's best malt,' he said.

The two men to whom Geigan had been talking were staring at the blood as it pooled into the dirt of the floor.

'Get him outside an' find an undertaker,' Hoke advised them. 'Best not to think of him as a friend if you step back in here.'

The men looked at each other. Geigan was a mess. He was shot to pieces and they were uncertain whether to carry or pull him from the saloon.

Hoke was about to tell them, when Sam Kluskey shouldered his way through the batwing doors. He was closely followed by his deputies, Dixie Tennon and Jack Lambeth.

The sheriff immediately saw the body. From the grouping in the saloon, the set-up was obvious. He turned to Hoke. 'You came back for this?' he demanded. 'You brought your anger an' killin' ways back into my town?' His eyes flashed angrily. 'Who the hell is this?' he asked, pointing his rifle at Geigan's body.

No one answered and he looked around the saloon. 'Who saw the shootin?' he demanded, with an intolerant edge to his voice.

Hoke thought of reaching for his Colt, but once again ceded to the threat of Tennon and Lambeth.

The man standing closest to Geigan spoke up. 'We saw what happened, Sheriff. This feller sure picked the wrong spot. What he was sayin' about John, was real provokin'.'

From there on, others joined in. They seemed pleased in their unanimous agreement of what had been fatally played out before them.

'So, it was John who shot him?' Kluskey pressed.

'But it weren't him pushin' for the fight, Sheriff. He laid his gun up ... on the counter, about where it is now.'

Jack Lambeth flinched and levelled his shotgun at Hoke. Sam Kluskey shook his head.

'If anythin', it looked to me like he was offerin' it up,' the man continued with his exaggeration.

The sheriff stared hard at Geigan's body, then he took a step towards Hoke. 'Yeah, I'm sure that's just how it looked,' he muttered. 'Hardly self-defence, but I could understand the provocation. I guess *extreme*, would account for four bullets,' he added with more sarcastic bite.

'He was one of a few men with a nasty habit o' comin' back at me, Sheriff,' Hoke offered as an explanation. 'It's a long story. Perhaps one day you'll indulge me ... let me tell you about it.'

Sam moved closer to Hoke. 'It was close

to murder, an' everyone here knows it,' he seethed. 'That man's so full o' lead he's comin' to pieces. I did have some sympathy for what happened to you, John, an' I don't know if this man figured in it. But if you don't clear Old Oak, it'll be *me* tellin' *you* about a goddamn wooden hill.'

Hoke looked deep into Sam's eyes. The fact that he was being run out of town by his own son was scary, freakish. He wanted desperately to say something to the effect, but he sensed the time and place to be far off, wondered if it always would be. 'I never wanted this to happen, Sheriff,' he said instead. 'God, if only you knew.'

'I know enough, an' I'm advisin' you to ride away now.'

'I ain't done any wrong by the law, Sheriff. You ain't got much of a reason to run me off.'

'You came back for Otis Pipe, like we both knew you would. This man just got in the way. So who else? It's Pipe you want, I can smell it on you.' Sam turned to look at his deputies, waved an arm to indicate getting Geigan removed.

Hoke reached carefully for his Colt. He stared at it for a moment, then pushed it back into his jacket.

'At this moment, Otis Pipe is entitled to the protection of the law, an' that's *me*,' Sam said. 'If anythin' happens to him.' He rapped the barrel of his rifle against the bar, left his sentence fated and unfinished.

Hoke pushed aside the empty beer glass, downed the whiskey. '...You'll come lookin' for me,' he concluded.

Sam was about to say something else, but held back. He turned on the men who'd stood gawping as Tennon and Lambeth struggled with Geigan. 'Help 'em, for Chris'sake,' he snapped.

Hoke turned away, looked tiredly into the mirror that ran behind the bar. He watched Sam step over Geigan's body and push his way out through the batwings. He thought how different all their lives might have been if Coral had stayed with Sam that fateful night.

20

Within a week, Hoke found his way out on to Milroy Peggler's land. He had nowhere else to go, and travelling through the winter snows was the sole preserve of bears and timber wolves.

He offered to work, to earn his keep in Old Oak until early spring. But it wasn't so tough, was precisely where he wanted to be. He was also close to his stretch of land, and the man who'd taken it from him.

Peggler did offer up 200 acres, but Hoke had his pride and turned it down. Besides, he wasn't for starting over. He'd had enough of land and owning things.

Late one night, they were sitting in the comfort of Peggler's farmhouse. There were Indian sashes and blankets hung on the walls, and a bearskin was spread across the floor. Hoke was sitting in a comfortable wing-back, rigging a tale as to why he was staying on. In turning down Peggler's offer of land, it was plain there was no purpose other than his wanting to keep an eye on Sam Kluskey.

'There's still somethin' needs to be settled, Milroy,' he said. 'You know it, Sam knows it, an' everyone who lives an' works along the creeks knows it. I'll be on my way when I've done.'

'Where to?' Peggler asked.

Hoke shrugged. 'East, then east again. Across the Rockies, maybe.'

'That'll be *after* you've killed Otis Pipe?' Peggler suggested, pensively.

'Certainly won't be *before*.' Hoke almost spat his response. 'I've got no family ... other than a son who don't even know me ... no job, no home an' no goddamn prospects. Pipe's close enough to the reason for all o' that. So yeah, it'll be *after* I've killed him.'

Most folk in and around Creek Country *did*

know that Hoke John would seek punishing damages from Otis Pipe. The gripping tale around Old Oak was that Pipe was prey to a persecuted and dangerous gun.

In the genuine hope of preventing a pointless death, Milroy Peggler went to see Sam Kluskey. Peggler was a rich, influential businessman, and his opinions counted. He tried to talk the sheriff into heading off Otis Pipe, but after listening to Peggler for only a matter of minutes, Sam reached for his Winchester. He left his office and stamped through the snow that layered the sidewalk. Peggler was distressed. He wanted to tell Sam Kluskey that Hoke John was his father, but he couldn't. He knew it wasn't his business, but he didn't really know why.

However, it wasn't Hoke John that Sam went looking for. As sheriff, he thought he'd sorted that, given plenty warning. He knew where Otis Pipe was, and it was him he turned his attention to.

The would-be land owner was still keeping out of sight at the end of town boarding-house. As soon as Sam slammed the door shut against the bitter cold, Miles Esham twitched his head in the direction of one of the upstairs rooms.

The moment Sam set eyes on Pipe, he knew the man realized his prospects.

'Is John comin' here? Is that what you've come to tell me?' Pipe slavered.

Sam gave a thin smile. Then, with one hand he dragged Pipe from the chair he'd been sitting in. 'If I had my way, Pipe, I'd break you in half,' he snarled. He pushed the tip of his Winchester hard against the bone of Pipe's chin. 'The law says I got to protect you, an' I'm havin' real trouble with it.'

'You can get me away from here,' Pipe declared.

'Not in this weather. We're stuck in town.'

'There's places safer than this goddamn room. Get me there.'

Sam stepped back with a disgusted look on his face. 'There ain't a safe place for you, Pipe. But there's two rooms back of Oak's

Swallow. Milroy Peggler says it's where Penny Pinches will be doin' her changin'. He says you can hole up there until she arrives.'

'Why's he say that? Why's he want to help me?'

Sam crossed the room, stared distractedly at the snowflakes as they brushed the window. 'Hoke John's had time to stew, an' he's just about full cooked. If he gets to you this time, he'll kill you for sure,' he said. 'Then the law will have to step in, an' that's somethin' that me an' Peggler really don't want to happen.' The sheriff turned slowly, his eyes narrowed. 'That's about the root of it, Pipe. Now get out o' here, before I forget I'm that law.'

Pipe's jaw dropped. 'You're comin' with me?' he asked, suddenly very panicky.

'Oh yeah, I'm comin'. I want to know exactly where you are. But your man ain't in town, yet. If he was, you'd be dead already.'

Ten minutes later, they went through Milroy Peggler's office into a storeroom back of the Oak's Swallow Saloon.

'From here, you're that bit nearer your new home. When the snow clears, you can ride out to see it,' Sam sneered.

Pipe looked around him. 'I'll be alone here?' he muttered fearfully.

Sam was contemptuous. 'There's no one who'd want to spend a bunk-matin' moment with you, Pipe' he said. 'My deputies will come over when we know what John intends to do.'

'He intends to kill me, for Chris'sakes,' Pipe erupted.

Sam had a sudden urge to put a bullet into Pipe, himself. He'd be safe enough. There was only Hoke John to blame. He turned on his heel and stood in the doorway. 'Lock the door an' keep real quiet,' he said. 'If you so much as break wind, he'll get a bullet into you.'

Milroy Peggler was book-keeping in his hardware emporium.

'I've put him where you said. I didn't

bother to check if he's safe enough,' Sam told him. 'Are you goin' to feed him? Unless it's a condemned breakfast, my office ain't runnin' to them luxuries.'

Peggler sat quietly, a little troubled, something on his mind. 'If you get it to him, I'll pay. Personally, I couldn't swallow spit with Hoke John lookin' for me.'

'If he turns up I'll have to stop him. You reckon he will?' Sam said.

'Yeah, an' you'll probably have to shoot him. You thought o' that, Sam?'

'I've warned him right enough. I'm beginnin' to think he wouldn't have wanted this any other way.'

Peggler swore, got quickly to his feet. He was getting red in the face, and his voice was breaking. 'He would've,' he started. 'An' before it's too late, someone's got to tell you how.'

Sam looked confusedly at Peggler. 'What are you talkin' about?'

'It's Hoke John, Sam. John ain't his real name: his name's Bannen.'

'Bannen?' Sam repeated the name. 'His name's Bannen?'

'Yeah. He's your father, Sam.' Peggler was in now, and thought best to carry on. 'That man he killed in the saloon ... he was one of those responsible for runnin' your ma an' pa off their land.'

For a moment, Sam stood silent and motionless. He gripped his rifle, tight. 'Who's Otis Pipe?' he asked firmly.

'The brother o' the man who sliced up that ear o' yours. *That's* why your pa shot him.' Peggler lowered his voice to little more than a whisper. 'It was a long time ago. Sam ... you couldn't've been much more'n knee high.'

'But I remember.' Sam leaned against Peggler's big desk. He pulled the collar of his coat up and the brim of his hat down. He opened the door to the snow-swept street. 'Must be goddamn fate,' he muttered. Then he walked into the cold, billowing whiteness.

With a lock turned and a bolt thrown, Otis

Pipe passed a fitful night in the Oak's Swallow. It was well after first light that Jack Lambeth reluctantly handed him a plate of breakfast.

Pipe found the daylight hours dragged slow. The strain increased, the not knowing if Sheriff Kluskey had detained or even got to Hoke John. The long night hours brought their own mysterious terrors. He listened to the muffled bar-room sounds, occasionally heard raised voices and snatches of laughter, but it afforded him little comfort. Eventually another night turned into day, and with an early breakfast, Lambeth had brought a single-page broadsheet. As Pipe scooped up his warm beans with the biscuit, he read of Penny Pinches and her first appearance in Old Oak. Two columns described her charms, carried a short tale of her life. There was even a clumsy illustration of her showing a long, stockinged leg and satin garter.

Pipe read the details avidly, studied the picture. For a while it took his mind off his own predicament. But he'd been deprived, and he felt a curious, untimely resentment when he realized there was a chance he wouldn't get to see her perform.

He lay full-length on the sofa, took turns in dozing and listening. It was sometime later the same afternoon that he heard loud noises from the bar room.

He guessed it was Miss Penny arriving, maybe sharing a drink or two before her evening performance. Rubbing his arms against the chill, he stamped around the room a few times. He'd go out and see her. And if Hoke John was there, he'd have to mingle with quite a few others, by the sound of it.

Thinking he'd be safe enough, Pipe unlocked the door to the office. As he stepped through the doorway, he froze when someone tapped gently on the door ahead of him, then shrank from the refrain of Penny Pinches' voice.

'Let me in there, feller. It's colder'n a witch's tit, out here.'

21

From Milroy Peggler's house it was nearly five miles into town. In the morning, Hoke had told Peggler he'd been thinking on his actions. He wasn't making any rash moves, but now it was mid-afternoon, and he'd got to the end of his deliberations. If he didn't do something quick, Otis Pipe would get clean away.

He rode silent and remote. It was difficult travelling, for the trail was hardly used. His mare had to flounder through deep, near impassable drifts and the temperature was still dropping. Old Oak was blanketed in silence as he rode in from the south end, but although it was still early, there were a few lights strung along the main street.

Leaving his mare outside the boarding-house, Hoke paid Miles Esham a visit. It took a short, plain request to find out where Otis Pipe was newly quartered.

Hoke walked further into town along the deserted sidewalk. Even allowing for the heavy snows, it was obvious that because of Penny Pinches there was a bigger crowd than usual gathering in the Oak's Swallow. Hoke turned down the side of the saloon, cautiously approached its narrow rear door. He paused for a moment, then tried the handle. Silent against the encrusted snow, the door opened into the saloon's store-room. Hoke made an acid smile. For all Pipe's caution, he'd not thought to lock the door behind him, only the one in front.

From where he was standing, Hoke could see a low light in the office that led off the storeroom. Silhouetted against the glow, Hoke could make out a blocky figure, and he guessed Pipe was listening to sounds from the bar.

It would have been easy to put a bullet into the man, likely the smart thing to do. Pipe would have, if the roles were reversed.

Hoke stepped forward cautiously around Pipe's sofa. He leaned against the inner wall and, pulling his Colt, pushed its long barrel against the glass. With his other hand he gripped the door handle and twisted it quickly.

Directly in front of Hoke there was a brighter lamp that shone from the top of a writing desk. As the wood of the door creaked, the figure turned sharply. But it was Penny Pinches who was alarmed, who shrank from Hoke's levelled Colt.

The sight of her took Hoke by surprise. 'Ma'am. I was expectin' someone else,' he faltered.

'An' I was expectin' some privacy. It's usually *me* who gets to say who visits me in my room,' Penny retorted.

Hoke didn't have much time to get the meaning of what the chanteuse was saying, and it was too late when he saw her eyes flick to a place behind him.

'Maybe it was me you were expectin', Mr Bannen ... or John, whatever your goddamn tag is. Drop the hogleg, and don't move. Don't even tremble.'

Pipe's words sliced into Hoke and he felt the gall flood his mouth. When he dropped the Colt, he knew he'd get a bullet from a despairing man. It was the certainty of it that made him shake his head, and that, too, was the wrong move.

Hoke knew that Pipe wasn't waiting until his Colt hit the floor, and he turned as Pipe pulled the trigger. The blast of the shot fused with the gulping cry of Penny Pinches, and Hoke instinctively hurled himself sideways. He saw Penny fall across the table, her body crushing the chimney of the oil-lamp on the desk.

The room turned to instant blackness, but in the afterglow the scene was indelibly stamped. Otis pipe stood with fearful eyes and a smoking gun. He was staring at Penny Pinches who was spread grotesquely before him. Against the white of her bodice she appeared to be gripping a bunch of crimson flowers.

190

Hoke heard the warning click of Pipe's gun hammer, but his mind had retained the scene within the room. In one brief movement he dropped his Colt and hurled himself forward. As his big hands grasped for the flesh and bone of Otis Pipe, his mind flashed back to Red Willow Creek, Coral and young Sam. A wildness pounded through him as he made contact, as he prepared for a final and merciless fight.

He gripped Pipe's gun-arm tight, smashed it left and right wildly until he heard the gun hit the floor. He let go for an instant and managed to hook his arm around Pipe's neck. He squeezed hard but got tripped and both men fell to the floor. Although in darkness, Hoke could tell he had the advantage. He was so close, he felt the man's dampness, and the peppery sweat stung his nostrils.

After the gunshot, Hoke was expecting someone to come crashing through the door. But they were alone, thrashing blind and wild. It was for survival and both of them knew it.

Hoke felt a brief slackness in Pipe before fingers tore cruelly at his face. He rolled on to his back and lashed out with his feet, at the same time grabbing and pulling with his hands. His feet made a more solid contact, and with a crash and splintering of glass, the door of the office flew open.

Locked together, the two men were turned into the far end of the bar room. The customers had heard Pipe's gunshot all right, but none of them was prepared to look into it. They were only interested enough to form a broad horseshoe around the door to the room Penny Pinches was using as her changing room.

Hoke quickly twisted away to give himself an advantage. Swearing excitedly, he pushed himself to his feet. Then he was up and running, his eyes sweeping challenge to the startled, frightened onlookers. He made the end of the long bar just as the bullet smashed into his leg above his left knee. He gasped at the pain, swore again. It was Pipe. He'd been carrying a belly-gun in the band of his pants.

Hoke threw himself behind the bar. The bartender paled and backed off, dropping his glass cloth. He held out his hands in fearful sufferance as Pipe's second bullet ripped into the barfront. As Hoke hit the floor, he pointed to the running-shelf along the inside-back of the bar. Hoke nodded, twisted up and made a grab for the sawn-off shotgun.

The bartender was now crouched at the far end of the bar. Hoke held up the gun and gave him a penetrating look. The bartender nodded convincingly and Hoke knew the shotgun was loaded. He got to his knees, flinched with pain as he poked the barrel over the bar. He tipped it upwards towards a cluster of lamps that was lighting the room and thumbed back the hammers.

'Burn in Hell, landgrabber,' he yelled, as he pulled one of the triggers.

The overhead lights went out in a down-pour of shattered glass and oil. As the boom from the shotgun reverberated around the saloon, Hoke aimed at the second cluster. He gave them the second barrel, and within moments the bar was suffused with the hot taint of oil. Those men that hadn't made it through the doors were cowering against the walls, their senses reeling from the conflict.

There were more cartridges in a cardboard box and Hoke reloaded. He looked up at the high shelves that ran along the back mirror. There were some cut glasses and they twinkled brightly under the one remaining cluster of hanging lights. Fancy labels adorned the bottles, and for an otherworldly moment, Hoke supposed business had got real good for Milroy Peggler. Then he wondered about Pipe. There was no more shooting, and he couldn't hear much above the background clamour.

Quickly, he lifted the shotgun again and pointed both barrels along the counter-top. This time there was real terror. Hoke felt it himself as the gun blasted, the buckshot sweeping everything from the counter, the yelling as a thousand fragments of glass and liquor overwhelmed the room.

In the confusion, Hoke pushed out from

the end of the bar. He swung the shotgun to where he guessed Pipe to be, but he wasn't there. The saloon was empty. Everyone had left. The batwing doors had stopped moving.

But he knew Pipe hadn't got out. This time it would be to the finish. Pipe wouldn't have wanted it that way, but he'd know it had to be, even know he wasn't getting out alive.

Hoke's leg was an unbearable mass of pain as he rolled his way back to behind the end of the bar. Now it was going to take more than a single shot, and he'd need another cartridge.

Pipe took the barrel of his belly-gun from hard against the bartender's neck and fired low along the back bar. He'd got into position and waited for Hoke, fired the instant he'd seen him.

The bullet drilled, burned into Hoke's shoulder and he went over. But Hoke had seen the flicker of movement. He'd already slammed the shotgun down into the crook of his arm and jerked at the twin triggers.

He fell on to his back and took a few shallow breaths. He didn't need look at what he'd shot.

Otis Pipe didn't feel any pain, he was beyond that. From such close range, Hoke's shot had destroyed most of his senses. But he could smell. Through the blood and gore that covered his face, the scent of Penny Pinches fluttered around the remains of his nose. It was a hideous fragment of reality, before agony hammered him into oblivion.

His face grey and sweating with pain, Hoke managed to change the spent cartridges. With his good leg he pushed himself away from the bar. He made it to the doorway of Peggler's office, could go no further. He twisted his head to look back into the room, dimly saw Penny Pinches' body slumped and unmoving across the littered desk.

Then he turned back to the bar room. He gritted his teeth, grinned darkly at the finger of flame. It was running towards the coal-oil that swelled thin and threatening across the floor of the saloon.

22

Miles Esham pushed open the door of the sheriff's office. He found Sam Kluskey and Milroy Peggler talking with the deputies. The heavy snows would keep any trouble off the street and they were sharing a drink before going to see Penny Pinches at the Oak's Swallow. It was at Peggler's invitation, and Sam was joshing, bending a proverb.

'It's truly an ill wind that blows nobody any good. I'm sure lookin' forward to seein' that garter o' Miss Pinches.'

Jack Lambeth chuckled. 'We'll go an' quieten 'em down before the show starts. Sounds like some of 'em are already shootin' the roof off Mr Peggler's saloon.'

The men looked up, grimaced at the snow-flakes and cold that blew in with Esham.

Sam eyed the man from the boarding-house. 'You been tryin' to overcharge again, Miles?' he asked, noticing the bruise under Esham's eye.

'Yeah, that's what I come to see you about. It was Hoke John. He would've done more if I hadn't told him.'

Short-lived content disappeared from the sheriff's face. 'Hoke John? You've seen him in town?'

Esham looked miffed at the lack of concern for his hurt. 'He came bustin' into my place ... wanted to know where Pipe was,' he answered.

'An' o' course you told him.'

Esham turned the bruised side of his face towards Sam. 'Yeah, I told him,' he said sourly.

Sam was out from behind his desk, reaching for a coat. 'When?' he asked anxiously.

'No more than an hour ago.'

Sam's face clouded over. 'An' it took you that long to get here?'

Peggler understood Sam's concern. 'You could have a death or two on your hands,' he snapped.

'Milroy, you come,' Sam said. 'I'm afraid o' what...' He stopped, changed the direction of his thoughts. 'It's your place, goddamnit,' he offered instead.

On the sidewalk outside his office, Sam stared through the falling snow. Away on his left, he saw two men staring across the street. One of them looked up and waved, jabbed his hand excitedly at Oak's Swallow.

Lambeth winked at Tennon. 'That shootin' weren't high jinks, Dixie. Hoke John's gone too far this time. I told Sam he's goin' to have to kill him.'

Sam swore, took off at a run and the others followed.

'A hundred dollars says you're wrong,' Peggler called out to Lambeth. 'Make it two ... five,' he added, taking advantage of what he knew about Hoke and Sam that Lambeth didn't.

Along the street there were a few oil lamps throwing eerie, yellow pools of light across the deep snow. The town appeared to be deserted, the only sound in the blue dark was the muffled thump of Sam's boots as he took the steps of the saloon.

As he burst through the swing doors, he saw his father through the sweep of orange flames. Hoke was at the far end of the saloon propped against the doorway. His head was back and he was staring up at the shattered lamp carriers.

'He's hurt, Sam. Where's Pipe?' Peggler was breathless as he pushed up behind the sheriff.

Sam pointed his rifle at Pipe's feet that poked from the near end of the bar. 'Destroyin' more land,' he said viciously.

He looked over at Hoke. 'Ain't goin' to be long before these flames get to you, Mr John. I told you about Pipe ... even gave you a couple o' days. Seems you're always givin' me problems.'

'What's your beef this time, Sheriff?' Hoke spoke quietly. His chin fell to his chest and his fingers let go of the shotgun.

'I don't know whether to leave you lyin'

there, or to come an' get you.'

'Oh yeah. That must be a real dilemma.'

Anxiously, Sam watched the flames spread further across the saloon. He turned to his deputies. 'Get round the back. You can reach him through Milroy's office,' he snarled.

'Where the hell's Miss Pinches?' Peggler shouted at Hoke. 'Have you seen her?'

'She never made it out o' your office, Milroy. Pipe made sure o' that.' Hoke tried an exasperated smile. 'That makes *him* the killer.'

Sam shook his head, looked at Peggler. 'I can take care o' this,' he said. 'Go get some help. Get a water chain goin' if you want to save this place from burnin' down.'

Peggler nodded thoughtfully and backed off through the swing doors.

'We're on our own, Sheriff. Make up your mind what you're goin' to do about me, before I burn to death,' Hoke croaked.

'I ain't goin' to shoot you, but maybe I should let you warm up a bit.' Sam took a step closer, held up his hand against the heat.

Through the hiss and rustle of the rising flames, he heard a short, gurgling chuckle.

'I knew Milroy would tell you, before *I* ever did,' Hoke answered him back. 'It was the timin' I was never any good at, Sam.'

Sam was wondering how long it would take Tennon and Lambeth to get to Hoke. 'You don't want to hang around there too long, old man. I'll give you time to get to your horse,' he came up with.

'In this weather, are you kiddin'?' Hoke called out. 'Anyways, I've lost so much blood, gettin' in the saddle would kill me. Besides,' he said, closing his eyes against the tiredness and pain, 'you don't really want me to leave now, do you, boy? Not now we've tamed this hell-raisin' town o' yours?'

'No. But I'll bury you alive if you call me boy again,' Sam said, as he saw his deputies appear through the back office.

23

Hoke John sat uncomfortably on a deck chair at the end of town. The gunshot wounds had been effectively doctored, but his whole body ached. It was still bitterly cold and he shivered under blankets and a fur skin.

The Oak's Swallow saloon had burned to the ground, and black charred stubs poked through the snow that still lay clean across the land. Some said the fire was God's reckoning; others that it gave Milroy Peggler an excuse to build a bigger, more elaborate saloon with a proper theatre and dance hall.

Sam Kluskey stood on the sidewalk, his arms wrapped around him against the chill. 'I don't rightly know what to call you ... now,' he stumbled through his sentence.

'Yeah, must be difficult. But *rightly,* it's still

Pa.' Hoke coughed, laughed, pulled at his blanket.

Sam stamped his feet. 'There was somethin' I meant to tell you,' he started. 'About that old dog o' yours...'

Hoke's eyes flickered. 'What about him?' he asked.

'When Lambeth went into your cabin that time he was dead. He said there was still some warm to him. Must've died the minute you left.'

Hoke stared into the distance, squinted at the brightness. 'Yeah. I know how he felt,' he said distractedly. 'Christ, ain't that sad.'

Sam nodded. 'Yeah,' he commiserated. 'A lot o' folk gathered for Miss Pinches. Must be a record for Old Oak.'

There was silence for a full minute before Hoke said anything else. 'Milroy ever tell you why she was called Penny Pinches?'

'Yeah, he did,' Sam answered.

There was another long pause, and Hoke tried again. 'I bet you don't remember what I told you about snow.'

Sam laughed. 'I do. A snow year's a rich year, you said.'

'Yeah, that's right. An' it's true enough.' Hoke sniffed loudly, stopped his mind from wandering back. 'We ain't got a lot to say, have we?' he added.

'I'd say there's plenty o' talk for some other time. Right now there's a heap o' work needs doin'. Some of it out on that stretch o' land, upriver. Take the two of us, I reckon.'

Hoke suddenly felt less cold. 'If it's the land I think you mean, you need remindin' it ain't mine,' he said.

'Yeah, it is,' Sam answered him. 'Otis Pipe left a confession somewhere. It was some sort o' last will and testament. Peggler's lookin' ... says he's sure to find it.'

Hoke understood and looked up at his son. He grinned. 'I'm sure he will. Milroy Peggler's an inventive an' resourceful man, if nothin' else.' After a moment, he went on to say, 'About Otis Pipe...'

'I know about him,' Sam checked in

quietly. 'Ma told me about him an' his brother.'

'Did you bury that old hound o' mine?' Hoke asked eventually, after another long silence.

'Yeah, I buried him for you. That an' a hatchet.'

The publishers hope that this book has given you enjoyable reading. Large Print Books are especially designed to be as easy to see and hold as possible. If you wish a complete list of our books please ask at your local library or write directly to:

Dales Large Print Books
Magna House, Long Preston,
Skipton, North Yorkshire.
BD23 4ND